RAW DEAL AT
THE END OF A RAWHIDE

Raider straightened and squared off facing Ralph. "Any time you're ready." He grinned.

But Ralph was grinning too.

Instead of charging toward Raider he stooped and snatched up the handle of the whip. The long lash snaked out behind him ready for its stinging snap.

Raider crossed his wrists in front of his eyes to protect them and balanced on the balls of his feet.

One cut. There was no way he could prevent the son of a bitch from getting one cut at him. But there might not be another. Not if Raider could get inside the lash faster than Ralph could back away from him.

Raider braced himself for the hot sting of the vicious lash and stepped forward...

J. D. HARDIN

THE RUNAWAY RANCHER

BERKLEY BOOKS, NEW YORK

THE RUNAWAY RANCHER

A Berkley Book/published by arrangement with
the author

PRINTING HISTORY
Berkley edition/March 1986

ISBN: 0-425-08665-8

A BERKLEY BOOK® TM 757,375
Berkley Books are published by The Berkley Publishing Group,
200 Madison Avenue, New York, N.Y. 10016.
The name "BERKLEY" and the stylized "B" with design are trademarks
belonging to Berkley Publishing Corporation.

PRINTED IN THE UNITED STATES OF AMERICA

CHAPTER ONE

Doc Weatherbee settled back in the seat, rolling his head to the side so he could look out the window at the countryside rolling past. The rhythmic *clack-cla-clack* of the train carriage wheels passing over the rail joints was hypnotic. He rather wished he *could* go to sleep. At least that would block out the noise of Raider's incessant bitching.

If it wasn't one thing it was another. The lunch the butcher boy had sold them out of his basket wasn't sitting well on his stomach. He had gas. The cigar smoke in the car was giving him a headache. Why the hell had Allan picked *them* for this particular job when Raider knew for a fact that Ben Rickard was closer to the meeting point' and was *not* due any free time.

"Rade, will you please shut up? Just for a little while? Please? I'm tired. I'd like to rest until we get there."

Raider nudged him in the ribs with a sharp-pointed elbow. "Had you a good time last night, huh?" He winked lewdly.

"I don't want to discuss it, Rade. Truly I don't."

Raider leered and winked again. "You don't have to tell me, pard. I could see the way she was lookin' at you. Pussy-whipped, that's what you are today." The man cackled loud enough to draw stares from other seats in the nearly full rail car.

1

Doc scowled at him briefly and closed his eyes, wishing he had the ability to close his ears as well because Raider would keep on talking whether Doc acknowledged the flow of words or not. Doc knew that. Escape was impossible. He sighed. The mere fact that Raider's speculation was correct did nothing to change Weatherbee's displeasure. The pleasantly hollow feeling deep in his groin did nothing now to make him feel more rested. He wanted to *sleep*, damn it, and there would not be much time left before they were scheduled to pull into the bustling station at Kansas City.

Doc kept his eyes closed, and Raider rambled on. Mostly complaining. Mostly cussing.

Eventually the train squealed and clattered its way to a halt. The sign nailed to the end of the loading platform read KANSAS CITY. Doc tried but could not remember at the moment whether the depot was on the Kansas or the Missouri side of the artificial line that bisected the sprawling city. Not that it mattered. He shook his head as he stood, trying without much success to ignore the flow of Raider's comments as they joined the other passengers filing out of the car and down the steel steps to the platform.

"Shit," Raider grumbled.

"What now?" Doc asked wearily.

"No brass band. You'd think at the very least, if we're so fucking valuable that they got to change all my plans, they'd at least have a brass band waiting for us. Maybe even some dancing girls."

Doc smiled and patted the tall, black-haired operative on the shoulder. "Have I ever told you, Rade, that you are a true joy to work beside?"

Raider looked startled for a moment. "Uh, no, I don't reckon you have."

Doc's smile grew wider. "Good." He turned back toward the baggage car to claim his things, leaving Raider to trail along behind.

They piled their gear into the back end of a hackney and climbed inside. Weatherbee gave the destination to the driver.

"The Fleur de Lis Hotel, if you please, sir," he said, giving the words the correct French pronunciation.

The cab driver turned on his seat and eyed them—Raider in particular—with a slightly raised eyebrow. Then he shrugged and shook his reins, sending the team away from the curb and into a smooth trot.

So the Fleur de Lis was a fancy spot, Doc thought. He had never heard of it before, certainly had never stayed there, but the driver's reaction had been indicative.

Doc glanced briefly to his left, toward the sight the hackney driver had been so unsure of when the hotel was mentioned.

Actually Doc had been so often in Raider's company that he rarely even noticed the man's usual costume any longer.

Raider was tall, well over six feet, with a horseman's broad shoulders and narrow hips. Black hair curled out from under the crown of a wide-brimmed and equally black Stetson hat, and a jet black mustache swept in ferocious curves over the tanned and leather-tough skin he had developed after years of exposure to the elements. He wore denim trousers and Middleton boots, and his brown leather jacket looked like it had been scrounged from someone's refuse pile twenty years ago. Doc shuddered with horror every time he noticed the jacket, which was one of the better reasons for not paying attention to it any longer because Raider was unduly fond of the awful thing and wore it whenever the weather was reasonably fair.

Weatherbee, in sharp contrast, was dressed appropriately for any of the finer hotels in the city. His Chesterfield coat was graced with a vicuña collar and lapels. His pearl gray derby had a curled brim, and his spats were immaculate despite the soot and cinder dangers of railroad travel. His person was quite as striking as Raider's, if not so ruggedly flamboyant. His features were well molded and appealingly regular, common enough to allow him to change his appearance drastically by the simple expedient of growing or removing facial hair. At the moment he was clean-shaven except for the bushy blond Burnside whiskers. He was not quite as tall as his companion and was more heavily built. This soft-looking blond city slicker with his fancy clothes looked like he'd be a pushover in a bout of serious fisticuffs.

In fact he was as tough as rawhide but preferred not to show it.

With a small, slightly devilish curl at the corner of his lips, Doc pulled an Old Virginia cheroot from his pocket and carefully trimmed off the twisted tip before he applied a flame to the end.

"Do you have to do that, damn it? We just got out of that stinking rail car, and now you're smoking up the air."

"I certainly didn't mean to bother you," Doc said politely. He leaned forward and raised the isinglass window on his side of the hack, which only served to blow the smoke into Raider's face.

The neighborhood the cabby took them to was quite elegant. The few shops or business establishments along the quiet streets were identified by very small-size gilt lettering on their windows or by small, well-polished brass plaques beside their doors. There were no garish signs hung out in this quarter.

The Fleur de Lis was set well back from the street and was surrounded by trimmed green lawns and towering trees. There was no sign or name whatsoever on the gateposts flanking the graveled driveway to the porticoed front, only a brass fleur-de-lis symbol. Obviously the management here felt that any further identification would have been unnecessary.

The hotel itself was not large, but it was elegant enough to draw a whistle of awed appreciation from Raider. "Shit, Doc, are we gonna stay here? At *Allan's* expense?"

His amazement was well taken. Allan Pinkerton was as tight with his purse as every Scotsman was cracked up to be. The head of the world's largest and most efficient detective agency might justifiably have been the model all tightwad Scots were patterned after.

"At the client's expense is more like it," Doc said as the hackney wheeled to the front of the hotel with a flourish of high-stepping hoofs and tinkling harness bells. "I already told you this is a special case to Allan. The missing man is a friend of his from the old days. Big wallah deal and all that."

Raider whistled again and stuck his head out the window so he could see better.

"Don't do that, Rade. It's embarrassing. You act like a schoolkid on recess."

"Yeah, but... *shit.*" He seemed to expect that the expletive would cover it all. As it did.

As soon as the hack was stopped, it was surrounded by a swarm of white-coated porters who quickly emptied the luggage boot and whisked Doc and Raider's things out of sight.

"Where the fuck..."

"Rade, it's okay," Doc said, taking his companion by the sleeve and forcibly pulling him away from pursuit of the porters. "It will all show up again in our rooms."

Raider grumbled some more but allowed himself to be led inside.

The lobby of the Fleur de Lis was small, dark, and overfurnished. Nearly every permanent surface of wall or ceiling had been carved, gilded, or both. The desk clerk was dressed in morning coat and batwing collar.

"Gentlemen?" he asked. Doc was impressed. The man was so good at his job that he did not even wince at Raider's shabby appearance.

"Weatherbee and Raider," Doc said.

"Of course, gentlemen. Welcome. Shall I announce your arrival now or would you prefer to, uh"—this time he did look in Raider's direction, although with no change in expression—"to freshen up first?"

"In half an hour, please," Doc said.

Raider had not said a word since they walked through the huge, carved doors at the entry. He was gaping from one side to the other.

"Trapping flies, Rade?"

"Huh? Oh." He shut his mouth, but he continued to stare at everything they passed as a liveried bellman led them to their rooms on the second floor of the hotel.

Doc tipped the bellman—he knew better than to leave that detail to Raider or they would be unwelcome within minutes of arrival—and accepted both keys.

"Son of a bitch, Doc. Look here. Our bags are already in the rooms. They even knew which stuff went where. How the hell do you figure that?"

"I couldn't possibly know," Doc said politely, although the differences in their attire extended to the differences in their choice of luggage. Raider's was nearly as ratty as his coat. Doc's only real amazement would have been if any error had been made by the porters.

"Shee-it," Raider said with pleasure as he examined the adjoining rooms.

The rooms were admittedly nice, although Doc had seen better. But none recently, he acknowledged.

Raider left his clothes stuffed in a suitcase where they were, while Doc occupied himself with removing his suits and other things and hanging them in the large, cedar-lined wardrobe.

"Not bad, huh?" Raider asked. He propped the heels of his boots on the edge of Doc's bed and leaned back in the plush upholstered armchair, lacing his fingers behind his neck.

"The question," Doc mused, "is what we are going to have to do to earn all this."

CHAPTER TWO

A boy wearing a high-buttoned scarlet coat and slippers with soft, whisper-quiet soles knocked on Weatherbee's door exactly thirty minutes after they left the lobby. He collected both of them and led them to Mrs. Angela Boatwright's suite. The boy seemed to accept Doc as a perfectly normal and ordinary guest of the Fleur de Lis, but his eyes kept cutting sideways toward the scarred and use-polished grips of the Remington revolver that rode at Raider's waist. He had been taught much too well to ask any questions, but his delighted and eager expression spoke volumes without words.

The lady was expecting them. She was ensconced—that was the only word for it—in the center of a plush love seat with her hands folded demurely in her lap, posed as carefully as if she were sitting for a portrait. The flowing yards of fabric in her gown and crinolines filled the full width of the love seat.

A pretty portrait it would have been, too, Raider thought when he saw the woman.

Mrs. Angela Boatwright was a handsome woman.

Her hair was polished jet, piled high in a confection of curls and swirls and curlicues. Her complexion beneath that dark gleam was pale, pale cream. Her eyes were dark and stunningly wide, with extraordinarily long lashes that curved prettily against a swell of apple dumpling cheek.

Her lips were full, very red, and very moist. Her nose, though a trifle sharp, had a long, straight, patrician line.

The form beneath that lovely and well-groomed face was as excellent as the rest of her. Ripe, rich fullnesses molded into deliciously attractive curves. Her gown was cut low enough to show that no artifice was necessary to complement that figure and to show as well that the creamy, unblemished purity of her skin texture extended as far as the eye could see.

Raider looked at her and felt an immediate rush of interest. This was one hell of a woman.

Her eyes met his for a moment, and he could have sworn that under the cool, refined exterior there was a smoldering fire, banked for the moment but impossible to extinguish.

His lips twisted in a knowing grin as Mrs. Boatwright turned her attention to Doc, accepting his greetings and a correct, formal bow over her gloved hand as if both were quite properly her due.

"A pleasure, I'm sure, Mr. Weatherbee," she said in a low, throaty voice. "And this...?" Her eyes returned to Raider, and her chin went up a fraction of an inch in a haughty gesture so that she could quite literally look down her nose at him.

Raider laughed and introduced himself. The grand lady, indeed, he thought. Bullshit. This one looked ready to go, for sure. He grinned and winked at her, but she pretended not to notice.

"Refreshments, gentlemen?"

Doc looked like he was willing to play her game, but Raider was not in the mood for it at the moment.

"Business first," he said. "Why'd you have us hauled down here so fast we didn't have time to stop for a good shit?"

"My apologies for—" Doc was trying to say, but the woman stopped him with an imperious lift of her fingertips.

She looked at Raider, and there was a slight twisting at the corners of Angela Boatwright's lovely lips. "You fancy yourself quite the ruffian, don't you, Mr. Raider? Crude. Boorish." She appraised him boldly, but there was a certain subdued sparkle deep in those dark eyes as she did so. "Tell me, sir, does all that muscle extend between your ears as well?"

"Really, Mrs. Boatwright—"

She cut Doc off again. "Allan has already informed me of his confidence in the pair of you, Mr. Weatherbee. There is no need for explanations."

"We were given only the most general of outlines about the case," Doc pressed, insistent on changing the subject. Allan Pinkerton had made his feelings clear about this one. In this matter his operatives were welcome to quit the agency, but under no circumstances were they to quit the case. John Boatwright was—or had been—a personal friend. Doc had gotten the impression that Allan felt some debt of gratitude to the man as well. This was Allan's opportunity to repay that debt. And Allan Pinkerton was as careful in the payment of debts as in their collection.

Whatever else happened, Weatherbee did not want Raider putting them off on a footing that would spell disaster before they ever got onto the investigation.

"We would appreciate hearing it fully," Doc persisted. "In your own words."

"Very well." Angela Boatwright took her time about rearranging her skirts, fluffing them over her lap and helping herself to a sip of some beverage from a tall, stemmed glass on the small table beside the love seat.

"My husband is missing. He and Carter Purvis and the remainder of the employees. With the exception, that is, of his man Charles, one of the workers at the ranch. I brought Charles with me, of course. I assume you shall want to question him. He is staying in the servants' quarters. I can ring for him if you like."

"In a minute," Doc said. "First we want to know what you can tell us."

Angela Boatwright shrugged, the merest suggestion of rise and fall of her creamy shoulders. "John and Carter are missing. They left home four months ago with a considerable herd of bovines. The animals were delivered to a man in Montana upon payment of cash for the purchase price. A great deal of money was involved. John wired me from Montana to say he would be returning by way of a town called Ogga . . . Oggall . . ."

"Ogallala?" Raider prompted.

She nodded. "Something silly like that. Yes. He had made arrangements in advance to deposit the cash with a bank there in exchange for a letter of credit payable on our own bank in Shreveport."

"I thought you were from Texas," Raider interrupted again.

She gave him a look as though he had just spoken a bad word—although she had not noticeably reacted earlier when he did cuss. "Some things, sir, are best done in the more civilized surroundings of Shreveport or New Orleans."

"Uh huh."

"As I was saying." She paused and gave Raider a cold look. "Arrangements had been made. He was to make the banking transaction in that Oga-something place and then return home by rail. They were expected last week. Neither John nor Carter returned. I have had no wires from either of them. They and the cash seem now to have disappeared. I contacted the officials at the bank. They say no transaction was made. They could, of course, be lying. Or some ill may have befallen John and Carter after the first wire was sent. It is your duty, gentlemen, to find them. And to find the money if they have been killed."

"What does this Charles know about it?" Doc asked.

"Charles was an employee. He accompanied them on the drive to Montana and returned home separately. He expected to be the last of the party to return. In fact, he is the only one who has done so."

"I see," Doc said.

"We'll want to talk to this Charles, of course," Raider said. "You said he was, is, an employee?"

Angela Boatwright nodded. "That is correct. A ranch worker."

For a woman whose man was a big-time cowman, Mrs.

Boatwright sure as hell didn't use any of the lingo, Raider noted. She acted like a ranch was just a more profitable kind of store or business enterprise. Employee, huh? There weren't a whole hell of a lot of cowhands who'd allow themselves to be called that. Not to their faces, anyhow. Most of those independent sons of bitches would spit in your eye and quit an outfit before they would let it be said that they were *employees*.

"I think," Doc said, "we should go see Charles now."

"I can ring for him, if you prefer," Angela Boatwright offered.

Doc shook his head. "He may be more comfortable—speak more freely, if you please—if you remain here while we interview him."

"Of course." Angela Boatwright took another sip of the beverage at her side and dismissed the two Pinkerton operatives.

Raider rolled his eyes and whistled softly again once they were out in the hallway of the hotel.

"Yeah," Doc said.

CHAPTER THREE

The servants' quarters where Charles was being housed were a double row of tiny cubicles, each with a cot, a washstand, and a steel mirror, built over the stables behind the Fleur de Lis.

Charles turned out to be Charlie Krepp, a youngster of eighteen or so with red hair, freckles, and a wide smile. He offered his hand first to Raider when they were introduced and seemed much more comfortable with him than with the much better dressed Weatherbee.

"C'mon in," he said with a smile. He welcomed them into his little room and gestured around the bare walls proudly. "Ain't this something? All to myself, too. Don't hafta share it with nobody." He winked. "Less I want to, that is." He flopped onto the cot at the head and motioned for Doc and Raider to sit as well.

"I expect I know why you boys are here," he said. "And I got to tell you it worries me as much as it does Miz Boatwright. It surely does."

"What can you tell us about it, Charlie?" Raider asked.

Charlie shrugged. "They was supposed to be back a week or better now, and they never showed. Can't say as I know much more'n that."

"Why weren't you with them for the return trip?" Doc asked.

"That was planned way back last fall when John, he got the contract with that Mr. Timmons to deliver the herd. See, I got me a sister lives in Denver. That's in Colorado, south of Montana. So when I heard we was going up the trail to the north country, I asked John could I come home round-about and stop to see my sister. I hadn't seen her since she got married an' went off with her man."

"You did that, then?"

"Sure. Had us a nice visit." He grinned. "An' that Denver, it's a helluva town, let me tell you. Saw a niece an' a nephew I'd never seen before and talked plenty. Then I come on home. I expected the other boys would be there already, but they never showed. So now here I am with Miz Boatwright to help look for 'em."

"Where did you see the crew last, Charlie?"

"At the Timmons' place."

"Where's that?" Raider asked. He frowned. Doc was taking one of those stinking cheroots out of his pocket, and there wasn't ventilation worth a shit in this room.

"That's up in the Musselshell country, south of the Missoura. Nearest town is Wolf Point, I think. It was to the ranch we delivered the cows, though, and that's where we split. The rest of the crowd was coming back down pretty much the way we'd went up, and I come, swinging down to the Belle Fourche and around those hills, then down to the Blue and along it to the Ogallala an' the South Platte. I had to hit the South Platte too, of course, but way the hell upriver from Ogallala." He shook his head with wonder. "Man, I never seen anything like them mounteens they got off to the west from Denver. Did you ever see the like?"

Raider shook his head in agreement with the boy, who must have just had his first experience at seeing country that stood on its ends.

"Tell us about the herd," Doc prompted, "and about the crew, Timmons, everything you can think of."

"Okay." Charlie sat back with his fingers laced over one knee and thought for a moment. "Helluva big herd, it was.

Like to stripped John of his cattle, but he said at the price Timmons was offering we could afford to restock ourselves when we got back. Nine thousand head, it was, divided into three divisions for trailing, about three thousand each, which is all a fellow'd want to handle in one bunch."

"They weren't all steers being taken north to fatten, then?" Raider asked.

"Naw, we couldn't of put up that many steers if we'd stripped the whole county to get them. This was a mixed herd. Stockers. Mostly cows and young stuff, in fact, with a few range bulls throwed in. Timmons wasn't so much interested in the bulls or steers. He said something about bringing in his own bulls to upgrade, but he'd contracted for the mixed herd and took all that was delivered."

"Nine thousand head," Weatherbee mused. "Mrs. Boatwright wasn't kidding about the amount of cash being large."

"Large? Shit, I mean to tell you. Twenty-seven dollars a head, though o' course the calves was throwed in for free. Wasn't but a few hundred calves at the most, though. They couldn't of stood the trip, so we left all of them home in Texas as we could wean off the cows."

Raider tried to do a quick calculation of the amount involved. Doc reached it first and said, "That's almost a quarter of a million dollars."

"Is it really? Shit, I knew it was a lot, but I never ciphered it out to that much. Damn."

"How was the money paid?"Doc asked.

"On the barrelhead," Charlie said. "A big ol' satchel full of it."

"One satchel? That doesn't sound right. That much hard money would take a pack train to carry."

Charlie shook his head. "Folding money it was, not hard." He grinned. "When he paid us off, John gave me a hundred-dollar bill to put in my pocket. I'd never seen one of them before, but I had one of my own for a while there." He laughed. "Sonuvabitch is gone now, but I sure had me one for a spell."

"Go on," Doc prompted.

"Well, there ain't all that much more I know. John got

his price, after we sat there a few days and waited for
Timmons to bring it down from some bank or other, as he
hadn't known exactly when we'd get the cows there, and
then John paid us off an' I took off straight for Denver.
That was in the afternoon. The rest of the boys was supposed
to lay over for the night and line out for Ogallala come
daybreak."

"How many in the crew?" Doc asked.

"Let's see now," Charlie mused. "There was some boys
that'd been hired just for the drive, and John'd give them
their wages right after we got there, before Timmons brought
the money down. So all that was left was the regular crowd
from home. That'd be Carter Purvis and the segundo. His
name is Abe. And Bert and Kyle and Leon and—"

"How many all told?" Doc asked. "Including John Boatwright."

Charlie counted on his fingers. "Nine. Not counting me
or the boys that had been hired temporary."

Weatherbee nodded.

"What about the remuda?" Raider asked.

"Sold them to Timmons exccpt what we was all riding
at the time. Easier that way than trying to trail them all the
way back home."

"And the cook wagon?" Doc was still looking for anything he could describe when they went asking questions
about the missing men along the planned route of march.

"Never had one," Charlie said. "Coosie cooked out o'
packs the whole way. Not so convenient in the easy country,
but a mule is a damn sight easier to get across a bad river
than some wagon. And a mule don't slip tires or break
spokes. Coosie was one of those that was along just for the
drive, and he collected his pay an' took off soon as we got
to where Timmons' cookhouse could tend to us. That's what
he does, see. Hires out to one drive after another, as many
as he can get in a season, and lays up the rest of the year
down in Laredo where he's always got some Mex chiquita
to cook his beans an' haul his ashes for him."

"I want you to give some thought to this question, Charlie, and write it all down for us. We will need a complete

description of each of the men, everything you can remember about what they might have been wearing, and a description of each of the horses they kept for the return trip."

"I reckon I can come up with all that, but I won't be able to write it all down for you. That, uh, that's something I ain't had time to learn yet. I figure to get around to it, though."

Doc stood. "I'll tell you what, then, Charlie. You give that some thought, and tonight one of us will come back and set it down on paper while you tell us. Okay?"

"Sure thing, Mr. Weatherbee. Anything I can do to help, I'll sure do 'er."

Raider and Doc let themselves out of the tiny room of which Charlie was so proud and walked back to the hotel building.

"Hell of a lot of money," Raider said.

"And a temptation to go with every dollar," Doc agreed.

"His own crew coulda plucked him. Or that fellow who paid over all that cash could of decided it was too much to let go of."

"And there is always the bank at Ogallala. They were expecting delivery of the money, just as Timmons was expecting delivery of the cattle."

"I'd say we got enough folks to be suspicious of," Raider said.

"And more than enough reason for any of them to have done murder."

"Kinda makes you think Miz Boatwright's a widow woman now, don't it?"

"It does for a fact."

They walked on in the twilight, the smells of cooking foods and fine sauces reaching them from the kitchen at the back of the hotel. Raider's stomach began to growl.

CHAPTER FOUR

Raider lay on top of the covers, propped up on both of the big pillows, shoes kicked off and jacket tossed onto the bedside chair. Except for that, he was dressed. He was wondering what would happen if he rang for the chambermaid. Except, damn it, he had seen the one that was on duty earlier. With his kind of luck she would still be the one on duty.

What he was *trying* to do was *not* to think about Mrs. Angela Boatwright, who was lush and horny and very likely a widow some weeks ago. And probably knew it.

He scowled at the ceiling and thought that with a rich bitch like that one, she would probably go for that damned Weatherbee, anyway, with his highfalutin airs and fancy clothes. He would be just her type. Mrs. Boatwright had done everything but ask where the bad smell was coming from when she looked at Raider.

Bitch!

He didn't want to think about the woman, he told himself that he wasn't going to anymore, but he kept on doing it anyway.

Bitch.

He heard a light knocking at the hall door. The other door, the one that connected his room with Weatherbee's, was also closed.

Probably Doc back from taking dictation from Charlie, Raider thought.

"Come in, you old fuck," he called. "It isn't locked."

The door swung open and Angela Boatwright came into the hotel room.

She was smiling.

"I'm not old," she said.

Raider had been thinking about her so much, thinking about the size and shape and texture of those half-exposed breasts, that now that she was in the room he was hardly surprised at all.

He had, however, been thinking of her as a bitch so much that he was still thinking of her that way.

"What's the matter?" he asked in a sarcastic tone. "No answer next door. Or do you get your kicks by teasing? P.T., they call that. Prick tease. I don't like a prick teaser."

Angela ignored him. She turned with a swish of swirling skirts and locked the hall door, then crossed the room and turned the key in the door to Doc's room as well.

When she faced him again there was a smile tickling the corners of her mouth.

She came to the side of the bed and sat on it with her back to Raider, one hand falling lightly to his crotch. She squeezed gently there.

"Undo me," she ordered.

"What?"

"I said—"

"I heard what you said, but you forgot something."

"What's that?"

He was still half angry with her as the result of his own thoughts. "You forgot to say 'please.'"

Angela whirled to look at him. There was surprise in her eyes. But not the anger he had expected. The smile licked at the corners of her full red lips again.

"Undo me. Please." She squeezed and kneaded at his cock. It was throbbing hard now under her touch, and she kept running her hand up and down the length of him under the cloth that covered him.

Raider grunted and sat up. He started at the top of the

long line of tiny buttons, flipping them free, gradually exposing more and more of a flawless back.

Angela took her hand from him and stood, cupping both her hands to the front of her gown. She turned to face him.

When she let go of the bodice of the gown, the soft cloth fell away from her, dropping to the floor.

She wasn't wearing anything beneath the gown and the crinolines that fell with it.

Her body was the kind a sculptor would choose as an ideal model for classic art. Full of breast, narrow of waist, wide of hip, with full, solid thighs and an inky tangle of dark hair in her vee.

She was smiling. She posed for him, standing first with one leg forward, then the other. Turning so he could see her better. Obviously receiving a form of gratification from the expression in his eyes.

"Well?" The single word was throaty, almost choked with her own desire. He could see droplets of moisture clinging to the hairs below her mound and chuckled when he remembered his first estimation of her: she was ready, all right.

Raider kept his face in a poker set. "The conformation is okay," he said slowly, "but that ain't worth a damn without performance."

Angela licked her lips and let her eyes droop half shut. "You've never had better," she whispered.

Raider shrugged. "Words," he said. "Bullshit." He faked a yawn. "Anybody can talk."

For the first time anger flickered over Angela's pretty face. It was there only briefly. She mastered it, and the smile returned. This time, though, the smile did not touch her eyes, only her mouth. "You seem to be the one who insists on talking," she said. "Or don't you like women?"

Raider laughed.

He stood. Most women he towered over. Angela Boatwright could look him in the eyes without having to tip her head back. He had not realized what a tall woman she was. She leaned forward, deliberately dragging her nipples over the cloth of his shirt. She sucked in a quick, sharp intake of breath and did it again. Her nipples were large and so red he suspected she colored them with something.

She made no effort to help him out of his clothing but stood and watched him in much the same way he had seen good stockmen assess the conformation of a fine bull or an outstanding stallion in the sales ring. Her eyes narrowed with intense concentration as she judged the power in his shoulders and chest, the hardness of his stomach, the strength in his thighs.

Mostly, though, she looked at the shaft that extended up and forward from his groin. It was so fully engorged that the head took on a gleaming shine from being stretched so tight, and every heartbeat caused it to bob and bounce a little. Angela licked her lips again and raised her eyes to meet his.

Raider bucked his gunbelt together and hung it over the bedpost, then pulled the covers down and lay on the bed. He motioned her to join him.

Instead Angela smiled, a slow, mysterious smile, and reached up to the back of her head. She pulled out a pin, then another. She took her time about it. The effect on her breasts was delightful, as she would have known full well. The lift of her arms pulled the skin tight under her breasts, raising them, pointing them. Raider found his eyes drawn to them, his desire for her intensified.

She removed the last of the pins and dropped them onto the table, then shook her head. The piled hair fell apart, cascading down her back to the crack of her ass. She smiled and raised her arms. Stretching. Posing.

Raider thought that if she didn't get into the bed, and get him into her, very soon, he would go ahead and spurt all over the damned sheets. He was becoming that worked up.

Angela moved forward with slow, catlike grace. She knelt on the side of the bed and swung one sleek thigh over his waist to straddle him.

Raider hefted her tits, one on the palm of each hand. They felt warm and solid. He ran his thumbs over the tips of her nipples, and Angela tilted her head back and closed her eyes. Her breathing quickened.

She lowered herself over him, pressing the lips of her sex down on the side of his shaft, trapping it between her crotch and his belly and dragging herself back and forward over it. She began to moan and to rock her hips from side to side while she continued to rub herself over him.

Raider let go of her breasts and took her by the hips, trying to position her so that he could enter. He wanted inside that. He wanted inside it *now*.

Angela shook her head vigorously from side to side and pulled away from him. "Not yet,"she said. "My tits. Squeeze them. Hard."

He did, and once again she lowered herself so she could rub the warm, wet lips of her pussy over him. She sighed.

"Now the tongue," she said. She moved forward on her knees, still straddling him, so that her crotch was poised over Raider's head.

When he didn't immediately respond, she lowered herself to him, pressing herself against him and rubbing his mustache and nose the way she had just rubbed his cock over herself.

"Hurry," she urged.

She positioned the tiny button of her pleasure at his lips and wriggled tight against him.

What the shit, Raider thought. Still, just this once. He nibbled at her. Within seconds she contracted and shuddered, the waves of pleasure washing through her.

"Ah. Ahhhh-h-h-h!" She sighed deeply and fell back away from him, lying on her back with his unsatisified cock pressing between her shoulderblades.

After a moment she moved to the side enough to allow his erection to spring up past her shoulder, through the thick mass of black hair, to stand tall and firm beside her round cheek.

She turned her head to the side and bit and ran the tip of her tongue over him.

Now they were getting somewhere, Raider thought. He closed his eyes and enjoyed the feel of it.

Angela turned onto her side, still draped over his body,

and propped herself on one elbow that was planted between his legs. With lip and tongue and free hand she caressed him.

But the damned woman was fixing to drive him out of his mind. Not once did she actually take him inside her mouth. She teased and nipped and nibbled, but not once did he feel the heat of the inside of her.

"Come on, damn it," he muttered.

"Not yet," she whispered.

"Yes, damn it."

She pulled away from him. "Do me again first," she said.

Raider pushed her away. "Are you going to do me or what?" he asked peevishly.

"Do me again," she said. "Then I'll do you."

Raider looked at her. The thoughts he had been having about her before her arrival came back to him. "P.T.," he said.

"No."

He sat up, as much angry with her as wanting her now, and rolled her off him. She lay sprawled on the bed, still clutching at him with one hand.

He turned and knelt between her legs.

"I'm not ready yet," she protested.

"Bullshit."

Angela slapped him, a hard, stinging sweep of her open hand across the side of his face.

Raider laughed at her and captured her wrist in his hand. She tried to slap him again with the other hand, but he pinned that too, holding both her wrists against the bed beside the black flow of her shiny hair.

"Bastard," she hissed.

"Bitch," he shot back.

She tried to writhe away from him, but he already had her thighs jammed apart.

He lowered himself to her, his pulsing cock finding the wet, gaping entrance it sought and plunging deep to fill her.

"You're hurting me."

He laughed. She could say whatever she liked. But he

could clearly feel the responses as her own body betrayed her, taking him and arching her hips upward in search of more.

"Bastard," she said again.

"Uh huh." He let go of her wrists, and her arms went around him, pulling him to her, holding him and drawing him ever deeper.

"Bastard."

He didn't answer this time. He only began to move. Slowly at first. Not wanting it to end so soon.

Angela pumped and bucked under him, slapping her belly against his and crying out with pleasure every time he thrust himself into her, sighing at every withdrawal, increasing the speed and demanding satisfaction from him.

Ready as he was, she reached her climax even quicker. He followed scant seconds later, pouring a hot stream of fluid into her.

She collapsed under him, her body going limp, her head rolling from side to side. She moaned and ran her hands over his back.

Raider lay on top of her, still socketed deep inside her. The first had been good enough to call for seconds.

"You bastard," Angela whispered after several minutes of rest.

"Yes," Raider agreed. "And you are a bitch."

"You aren't through, are you?"

He shook his head.

"Damn right you aren't, because I have plans."

"Fuck your plans."

"If you plan to fuck me again, you bastard, you'll do what I say."

Raider snorted. He felt a little uneasy, too. This was one strange woman. Demanding. Caring only about what she got, not what she could give.

He felt a bit like a piece of meat. As if Angela Boatwright would be quite as happy if she had only his cock to diddle herself with and could dispense with the rest of him entirely.

He was still inside her, and as he felt his erection return

to life he began to thrust slowly in and out of her dripping, overheated body.

He almost wanted to leave her. Just to pull out and walk away. Let her get herself off if that was what she wanted.

But he didn't do it. Her beauty and the lush caverns of that superb body had him in their grasp, and he stayed with her. Taking her. But being used by her too.

"Bitch," he said as Angela, a knowing, smirking smile on her lips, wrapped her arms tight around him and pulled him deeper and ever deeper inside her body.

CHAPTER FIVE

"I don't like that woman," Raider said with a shake of his head. He took a mouthful of the egg concoction they had been served and looked like he wanted to spit. "What *is* this stuff?"

"Hollandaise sauce," Doc said, sampling it. He smiled. "A good one, too."

Raider grunted and took another bite. He chewed skeptically, quite willing to dislike the strange stuff. In truth it was better than it looked. His primary objection was that it was something unfamiliar and therefore suspect. "Well, I reckon it won't kill me."

"Why don't you like Mrs. Boatwright?"

Raider shook his head, refusing to answer. He concentrated instead on the breakfast.

"Something that happened last night?"

"Nothing happened last night," Raider mumbled around a mouthful of the eggs Benedict.

That was a lie, of course. In fact he was not just whipped this morning, he was positively sore. The damned woman had stayed nearly until dawn, and she hadn't let either of them rest for a moment of that time. She hadn't shown up for breakfast, and Raider really didn't expect to see her again until sometime past noon.

"When, uh, I came back from Charlie's room last night," Doc said, "I was going to go over the descriptions with you." He smiled slightly. "You must have been groaning in your sleep. And I think your voice has gotten higher."

Raider shrugged. He seemed not at all upset about being caught in that kind of fabrication.

"Is there anything I should know?"

Raider shrugged again. "She's just . . . I don't know." Nor did he. It was nothing he could put his finger on. It was just a feeling. Indefinite. Too vague to describe. But too strong to ignore. "There's something about her that ain't right. You know?"

Weatherbee pursed his lips and exhaled slowly. "Not really. But I couldn't help noticing yesterday that she mentioned the missing Carter Purvis every bit as much as she did her husband."

"And the money," Raider said.

"That's only to be expected. Almost a quarter of a million dollars. But this Purvis was the only name she gave us when it came to the men, and she used it often."

"Employees," Raider corrected.

"Yes. Employees."

"Purvis is the ramrod, right?"

Doc nodded. "Charlie says Purvis has been with John Boatwright a long time. None of the men liked him."

"Liked," Raider repeated. "You talk like he's dead."

"I think we're both assuming that they are all dead. Or do you know something that I don't?"

"No." Raider finished cleaning his plate and looked around for a waiter. "You know, for funny-looking shit, this stuff ain't half bad."

"Why don't you have some more?"

"Good idea. I think I will." A waiter appeared at Raider's elbow almost immediately, and he ordered his second helping of the breakfast. "How do you reckon we should handle this one?" Raider asked when the waiter was gone.

Doc shrugged. "Park Mrs. Boatwright and Charlie here, or in Ogallala if it makes her feel closer to the investigation, and go on from there, I suppose."

"All right. That's the way it'll be, then."

"No!" Angela Boatwright was forceful to the point of fury. "I will *not* be treated like this. I will *not* be shoved into some convenient corner while you two incompetents pretend to search for Car . . . for my husband."

"Mrs. Boatwright. Please. Be reasonable." Doc spread his hands in an appeal for understanding and put on his most reasonable expression. "An investigation, particularly an investigation into matters that may be, uh, criminal in nature, is a matter of some delicacy. Confidentiality. Surely you understand that—"

"I'll tell you what I understand, Mr. Weatherbee," she snapped. "I understand that I have already sent a wire to my husband's old and dear friend Mr. Pinkerton. Would you care to see his reply, sir?" Her manner clearly implied that the war had been won before the first shots were fired. She opened her handbag and triumphantly pulled out a fold of yellow paper.

Doc sighed and accepted the message form. It was addressed to Mrs. John Boatwright, Fleur de Lis Hotel, Kansas City.

INFORM OPERATIVES YOUR WISHES TO BE MET STOP
NO EXCEPTIONS STOP MATTER URGENT STOP ALL SPEED
REQUIRED STOP NO EFFORT SPARED TO FIND JOHN STOP

It was signed by Allan Pinkerton himself.

"This isn't the way I would have liked to do it," Doc said with resignation, "but it looks like the best way out. You don't like the woman, but I think I can get along with her. After a fashion, anyway. So I'll take her with me. We'll head for Ogallala by train and hire transportation there. Horses if she can ride. A rig if she can't. And start up the trail the way the Boatwright crew was supposed to be coming down from the Timmons place. Someone should have seen them along the way."

Raider nodded.

"Meanwhile, you go on up to see Timmons. I still believe he is our most likely suspect in the disappearance, at least until or unless we learn differently." He pulled a sheet of paper from his inside coat pocket and handed it to Raider. I've copied off the descriptions Charlie gave me, but they are sketchy at best. What I would suggest, Rade, is for you to take Charlie with you and start from the Timmons end of it, then work your way back down the trail. We'll meet somewhere in the middle and see what we have to go on then."

"Why the hell should I take a wetnose cowboy with me? The kid'll just get in the way, and you know it, you old bastard."

"Would you rather take Mrs. Boatwright with you?"

"That ain't the point, and you know it, Doc."

"No, but there are a few valid reasons why Charlie should be with you. For one thing, he would be available to answer questions about the people and the activities on the scene without having to resort to telegraphed messages. He could expand on the descriptions as you need." Doc smiled. "And there might be some little shock value when this Timmons sees a member of the Boatwright crew standing in front of him. Assuming, that is, that he has reason to believe them all already dead."

Raider rubbed his chin and chewed it over. "All right, · damn it. You handle the woman. I'll take the kid."

"And we meet in the middle," Doc said.

"Sure sounds simple."

"Meanwhile, Rade, do remember to keep Allan informed of your progress at every step of the way. You know how he is about the report procedures. By the book this time, Rade. All right?"

"Sure, sure. By the book, Doc. Everything by the damned book."

Weatherbee shook his head. He knew Raider all too well to believe he was going to start paying attention to the book now. He never had before. So why start now? As always, the burden of trying to appease the home office while an investigation was in progress would have to fall on Doc's shoulders, and this one would be no exception, regardless of what Allan demanded in his telegrams.

"We'll split up and leave in the morning, then," Doc said.

"Yeah, an' by the time you catch up to me and the kid, I'll have the whole damn thing wrapped up. Have to do all the real work myself. As usual."

"Bullshit," Doc said gently. He reached into his pocket for a cheroot and was rewarded with a flicker of displeasure that thinned Raider's lips.

"Think I'll go for a walk now," Raider said as he quickly got up and fled from the elegant hotel room before Weatherbee could get a match struck and the cigar alight.

CHAPTER SIX

"Fast packet" was what *they* called it. Piece of floating shit was what Raider called it. Worse, he was sure that the miserable thing was going to vibrate itself to pieces at any moment. Without warning. Probably his body would be discovered in a month or two, downstream somewhere, fish-chewed and falling to pieces.

The boat was a long, slab-sided, impressively ugly shallow-draft sidewheeler that consisted mainly of a flat bottom with doubtful-looking sideboards, a leaky steam boiler plunked into the middle, and a deckhouse that was little more than a wooden shack nailed onto the flat bottom of the contraption. Any comparison between this rickety rig and one of the Mississippi River floating palace sternwheelers would have been laughable.

On the other hand, one of those huge and luxurious sternwheelers could not navigate the Missouri for more than a few miles past K.C. And then only when the water conditions were right.

This ugly little bastard was supposed to be able to make the trip hauling mail and light freight most of the year and faster than anything else known to man.

Raider damn well hoped so. Putting up with the discomforts of the outfit better be worth the effort.

The sleeping accommodations were whatever amount of deck space a man could find for himself, and no meals were provided. If a passenger wanted to eat, that was his own personal, private affair and no concern of the captain.

Captain, Raider thought with a derisive snort. The captain of the vessel was a round-bellied greaseball with last week's gravy still in his beard and the smell of cheap whiskey preceding him by a half dozen feet whenever he moved. Which was not particularly often, thank goodness. Raider was convinced the man was going to pile them up on a clinker at the very next bend. So far he had believed that with every bend they had come to. The fact that it had not quite happened yet didn't ease his doubts by a fraction.

Miserable as Raider was finding this trip, Charlie Krepp was in his glory. He had never been on any kind of boat before, and he found the *Sadie Marie* to be quite as grand as he had thought the servants' quarters of the Fleur de Lis. He spent most of his time standing in the prow of the boat with his nose lifted into the wind of her passage and a broad grin on his face. Every few minutes he would turn and trot back across the few available yards of open deck space to where Raider was reclining on a bale of yard goods and report on whatever new and wonderful thing he had just spotted in the distance.

Raider took one last survey of the other passengers gathered on the foredeck. They weren't much to see. Three slick-sleeved private soldiers with hangovers reporting back to someplace from someplace. A shady-looking gent with chin whiskers and long, pale fingers—no point in accepting *his* invitations for a card game to while the time away—and a young couple newly married and not hardly aware that there was anyone else in the whole damned boat. They had that smug look about them that said the two of them, personally, had just invented sex and weren't yet willing to share their discovery with the rest of the world.

Raider watched silently while the gambler finally succeeded in inveigling the soldiers into a card game and listened patiently while Charlie came trotting back to report to him that there was yet another wonder on the riverbank

ahead. Then he closed his eyes and tipped his hat forward
to shade his face. There wasn't shit worth seeing until they
got to Wolf Point, Montana.

"Where the hell have you been?" Raider grumbled. He
had been busy renting them a pair of horses—at an out-
rageous price that Allan Pinkerton was sure to bitch about,
especially when he saw that the agency was expected to
pick up the ticket for young Krepp's mount too—and Charlie had promptly disappeared.

The young cowboy grinned hugely. "Shoppin'," he said.
"Miz Boatwright, she gave me some travelin' money. So I
did me some shopping." He turned and proudly presented
his right side for Raider's inspection.

There, slung low on his hip in a shapeless leather pouch
that might once have been an army issue holster, or could
as easily have been originally intended for the storage of
nails, was the butt of a revolver. Not a new one either,
judging by the nicks and scars that were gouged into the
wooden grips.

"See?" He pulled it out of the pouch awkwardly and held
it up for Raider's inspection. It was a positively ancient Colt
1860 Army that had been a cap and ball revolver when it
left the factory but which had since, and none too expertly,
been converted to fire .44 rimfire cartridges.

With its backless construction and pinned frame, the old
gun was not even good for pounding nails, and if the kid
had paid more than fifty cents for it, holster included, he
had been robbed. Still, Charlie seemed so proud of the old
thing that Raider didn't have the heart to comment on it
except to smile and nod.

"What'd you do that for, Charlie?"

"We're going after a bunch of robbers and killers more'n
likely, ain't we?"

"Uh huh."

"Well?" He was still grinning.

Raider suppressed a groan. With his kind of luck he
would be the one who got a splinter of busted cylinder wall
in his ear the first time Charlie fired the damn thing. He

reminded himself to get the hell out of the way if he ever saw that thing leave its leather again. He looked toward the sky. It was coming evening, and they hadn't had a decent meal since they left Kansas City.

"It's too late to start down toward Timmons' place today," he said, "so let's hunt us up a place to stay and something to put in our bellies."

"Whatever you say, Rade," Charlie said with a grin. The kid had picked up the nickname from that damned incautious Weatherbee and seemed to delight in using it. Proved they were old buddies and pals, Raider guessed.

"Well, come on then," Raider said, this time suppressing a sigh as well as a groan. He was getting kind of used to that lately.

Raider was sitting quietly with a beer in front of him and a heavy meal lying warm in his belly. The buzz of a dozen or so conversations filled the smoky air inside the saloon, but none of them were particularly loud or intrusive. Charlie had wandered off to another table where a game of draw poker had been making up. Raider yawned.

The other customers in the place were a mixed bag of river runners, cowmen, and off-duty soldiers. There were no Indians inside the saloon, of course, but Raider was conscious of a fair number of dark eyes peering in through the front door and the two windows. There was a reservation somewhere to the north, he gathered, while the cattlemen were starting to fill up the country in all the other directions. Raider took another swallow of beer. It wasn't bad. There were certain advantages to being in a place where there was good transportation available from the big cities where the brewers worked.

"Cheat!" The single shouted word rang out sharp and loud over the other sounds in the saloon. It was followed by silence, broken only by the sound of a chair clattering onto the floor.

Raider looked. And swore softly to himself.

It wasn't Charlie Krepp who had done the shouting, but

it was damn sure Charlie that the spitting-mad cardplayer was staring at.

"Draw that thing, you little son of a bitch," the man yelled. He needn't have been so loud about it. There was not another sound in the place.

Charlie was sitting there with an uncomprehending look of shock on his freckled face. "But what...?"

"You been cheating us, you little bastard. And you know it."

"But I never...I swear I never..." He turned wide, moist, disbelieving eyes toward Raider, who was on his feet now and moving to the kid's side.

"What the hell is going on here, Charlie?" Raider asked.

The kid pointed mutely toward the man across the table from him. Fear made his mouth slack, and he had gone dead pale. "This man says I cheated him. But I never, Rade. I swear I didn't. I got real lucky. That's true enough. But I don't even know *how* to cheat nobody." He looked like he was ready to cry.

Raider looked at the other man and raised an eyebrow.

"The little sonuvabitch was bottom-dealing, mister," the man declared. He was barefoot and raggedly dressed. Raider guessed him to be a roustabout off one of the boats tied up at the wharf nearby. But while he might not have been wearing shoes, he was not completely undressed. The haft of a small knife stuck out of his waistband on one side and the grips of a small revolver on the other. And he was damn sure mad enough to start shooting.

"Calm down, mister," Raider said. "You caught him bottom-dealing, did you?"

The man's lips clamped tight for a moment. Then the anger poured through him again. "I know he was doing it," he declared.

"But you didn't actually *see* him do it?"

"You don't hafta see—"

"I never," Charlie wailed loudly. "I just got lucky there, a real good streak, and this man says—"

"I heard what he said," Raider put in calmly. He sighed.

"Take a look at him," he told the riverman. "Take a close look."

The man glared at Charlie. "So?"

"Hell, man, the kid ain't dry behind the ears yet. Where would he learn how to mechanic a deck o' cards?"

"How the fuck would I know where he'd learn it. I don't *care* where the little bastard learnt it. I just want my money back. An' right damn now or I'll put a bullet in his gizzard so quick he won't have time to holler before he dies. An' that's the truth, mister, I swear I will."

"Whoa up now, friend," Raider said. "Nobody likes to lose, but I think you better learn to take it better than this."

"I swear I—"

Raider moved closer to Charlie's side and stood facing the angry gambler. He didn't have to, but for the warning effect pulled the tail of his jacket away from the butt of his Remington. He smiled at the riverman. "What was it you were going to do, mister?"

The man glared again at Charlie, but only briefly. He was mostly looking at Raider now. And what he saw there was no wet-ear kid with freckles and fear on his face. Now he was facing a grown man with an easy confidence in his eyes. And likely more than enough experience to have put that confidence there.

The man swallowed. His eyes fell away from Raider's, and he seemed to be inspecting the grime under his toenails. "This ain't your fight, mister," he mumbled.

"Wrong again," Raider said.

The riverman stood like that for a few moments, looking down toward the floor, seeming to be thinking about something. Then he looked up again and met Raider's eyes.

"I don't figure to die for this," he said. "But I do reckon to get me some satisfaction out of it. 'Cause I still say this kid's a cheat and a liar. I *know* that, mister. You can't tell me different."

"All right. I won't try to tell you different."

"I'm gonna take this here gun outta my belt now. Two fingers. Real slow. I don't want you to make no mistake about what I'm doing."

"All right."

The man did. He pulled the revolver out very carefully—it turned out to be a .38 rimfire Smith and Wesson—and laid it aside on the table.

"Now," he declared. He rolled heavy shoulder muscles, flexing and loosening them. "Now, you little bastard." He looked toward Raider. "Or are you butting into this too."

"Nope," Raider said. "Charlie, pull your piece nice an' slow and lay it on the table there too. Fair is fair."

"But—"

"You sit in a game with the grown-ups, boy, you got to play the whole hand. That's the way it is."

Charlie gulped once but did as he was told. He fished the old Colt out of its pouch and laid it on the table.

The riverman grinned and lunged forward, charging clean through the table that was still between them.

Raider was surprised. So, likely, was everyone else in the place.

Charlie slid out of the chair and to the side before the riverman had time to reach him.

The riverman crashed into the chair Charlie had just been occupying, his fall helped along by a vicious backhanded swing of Charlie's clubbed fist that landed just over the larger man's ear. The riverman's face hit the back of the chair as he went down, and there was a good deal of bleeding going on all of a sudden.

The riverman tried to get up, but Charlie stepped in and stomped hard with the heel of his boot on the other man's bare toes.

The riverman screamed in pain, and Charlie chopped him in the throat, then stepped back and began to wing hard punches, left and right, over and over again, into the man's unprotected face.

The man went down to his knees and still Charlie kept punching.

"That's enough," Raider snapped when he saw young Krepp back up a pace and balance on his left foot, ready to snap the toe of his right boot into the riverman's face.

The kick started forward. Just in time, Raider stepped

in to throw an arm around Charlie's chest and pull the kid back off the beaten riverman. "That's enough, damn it!"

Charlie turned his head toward Raider. There was a wild, glazed look in his eyes, and he was already throwing a looping right toward Raider's jaw when he seemed finally to realize who had grabbed him. The punch halted in midair, and Charlie got a sheepish look of embarrassment about him. He blushed furiously and relaxed, turning it off as quickly and as unexpectedly as his fury had turned on. "I'm sorry, Rade. I didn't . . . I mean . . ."

"Okay. Okay. Back off now."

Raider looked down at the riverman. The man was bleeding heavily from a battered nose and mouth, and both his eyes were already beginning to swell. He was going to look like raw hell for a week or so.

"Rade."

"Uh huh?"

"I didn't cheat nobody. I swear I didn't. You just got to believe me about that." He looked and sounded utterly miserable at the thought that Raider could think otherwise.

"I believe you, kid. Now let's get out of here. We don't want trouble."

"Sure." Charlie got down on all fours and began to pick his winnings out of the sawdust on the floor where the table had been upended. The beaten riverman crawled out of his way while he did it.

When Charlie stood again he was grinning hugely and jingling a handful of gold coins in his fist. "I sure got lucky, didn't I?"

"Yeah," Raider said. "Lucky." He looked at the riverman, but neither he nor any of his friends seemed interested in any more trouble. The riverman was trying to stop the flow of blood from his face with a dirty kerchief.

"Lucky," Raider said again. He took Charlie by the elbow and steered him the hell out of there.

CHAPTER SEVEN

"C'mon, Rade. Gosh, I owe you anyway for the way you stood up for me back there. And I won that money. Fair and square, too. I was on a real streak." Charlie lowered his eyes and blushed slightly. "That was a real fine thing you did, standing up beside me like that, like we was real friends. I . . . I never had a real friend before I just *got* to show you how much I appreciate it. Please?"

Raider sighed. "Okay, Charlie."

"My treat? Please?" He looked as pleased and eager as a pup. He was practically squirming with excitement at the prospect.

"Aw, hell, Charlie. Okay."

The kid grinned and this time took Raider by the elbow. "C'mon, then. I already asked a fella before where we should go." He laughed. "Only one place here *to* go, so I hope it's nice."

"Whatever, Charlie." Raider allowed himself to be led away from the riverbank toward the edge of the town. The business district, such as it was, was left behind. They went past the last of the log homes and found a narrow but much used path.

"It's this way, I'm pretty sure," Charlie said. He seemed in a hurry.

Another minute of brisk walking brought them in sight of a long, low log structure with light showing through the windows. Behind the main building were a number of small, low-roofed shanties. One or two of these showed dim candlelight under their doors too.

"This?" Raider was already beginning to regret his acceptance of Charlie's invitation. The place didn't look promising.

"Yeah," Charlie said happily.

The freckle-faced kid led the way, grinning broadly when he entered the large building.

The place was one huge open room with a fireplace at each end and a crude bar set up against the back wall. The furnishings were a number of seedy-looking sofas scattered with no pattern or plan throughout the room. A drunk snored on one of them, and there was a bewhiskered bartender behind the keg-and-plank bar. Except for those two there were no males in sight.

There were women enough to make up for that lack, though. Six, no, seven of them, Raider counted.

The women wore loose-fitting chemises. And nothing else. They exposed their teeth in professional smiles as soon as Raider and Charlie entered, and they rushed to form up in a line at one end of the room, each of them posing to show off whatever she considered her foremost asset, whether it was breast, leg, or face. As far as Raider could see, none of them had all that much to brag about.

Charlie looked like he was ready to swoon at the sight of all that available womanflesh in front of him, though. He nudged Raider in the ribs and grinned. "Remember now. It's my treat." The grin got wider. "For my best friend ever."

Raider stifled a groan and humored the kid with a smile.

Charlie headed for the lineup of whores.

"Hey!" The barman crooked a finger, beckoning Charlie toward him.

"Yes, sir?"

"You don't touch nothing, kid, till I get the price of admission. Right?"

"Sure thing, sir." Charlie dug into his pocket for the money he had just won.

"Dollar apiece," the barman said, cackling at his own faint humor: *dollar apiece* or *dollar a piece*.

"For all night, sir? Or whatever of it we can use up?"

"Five dollars for that, kid."

"Yes, sir." Charlie plunked a ten-dollar eagle onto the bar. "That's for me and my best friend too," he declared.

The barman nodded and pocketed the coin. After the money was in his hands he smiled. "Take your pick, boys. Whatever of them you want. And if they give you any shit, let me know about it. I do my own whipping around here, so don't you go trying none of that yourselfs, hear?"

Charlie nodded. Raider ignored the barman and Charlie too. A thought struck him, and he snickered under his breath. If he ever got the chance, this might be *just* the place to bring old Weatherbee. It'd likely make old Doc's skin crawl to have one of these shabby-looking women playing with him. Raider wondered how he could work it so Doc would have no way to comfortably refuse. He'd have to give that some thought.

Weatherbee might not be in his element in a place like this, but Charlie Krepp sure was. The kid went romping up and down in front of the row of girls, ogling each of them in turn. Once or twice he paused to heft a floppy tit in his hand or to flip up the hem of a chemise and admire a dark bush. Raider was not a particularly fastidious man, but this crowd gave him visions of scabs and unwelcome livestock.

Charlie stepped back from the line he had already admired twice, grinned, and grabbed the wrist of a big blonde who had udders big enough to make a Holstein proud. He let out a whoop and looked back at Raider. "C'mon, Rade. We'll get shacks next t' each other, so hurry up an' make your pick. Though I already got the best one right here, eh?"

"She's a doozy, all right," Raider agreed.

A door set in the back wall opened and another girl came into the room, chin down and moving slowly. She was carrying a pail of water, which she set down behind the bar.

"Bitch," the barman said. "You're too fucking slow." He took a step toward the girl.

"Is that one part of the line?" Raider asked.

"Her?" The barman hooked a thumb toward the girl and shrugged. "I reckon, but I don't know why anybody'd want this skinny li'l thing when there's some real meat to choose from. But if you want her, go ahead. I don't give a shit."

"She's the one I want," Raider assured him.

The girl gave him a half-grateful, half-fearful look out of still lowered eyes and came to him.

He had not had time to really get a look at her before, but he could see now that the barman had been right about one thing. She was sure as hell a scrawny one.

Little bitty and with hardly an ounce of meat between bone and skin.

She had hair as dark as Angela Boatwright's but dull and lifeless in contrast with that glossy woman's glossy gleam of perfectly maintained coiffure.

She had dark skin as well and eyes to match. It was impossible to tell at the moment if she was a half-breed off the nearby reservation or possibly a Mexican set adrift in this northern country.

She was wearing the plain and much washed chemise that seemed to be customary here, but under it she was clean.

Nice enough looking, too, except for being so painfully thin. She put her hand delicately into Raider's but kept her eyes downcast.

"C'mon, Rade," Charlie said eagerly.

The kid hauled his chesty blonde out toward the row of cribs. Raider and his girl followed along behind.

"Over here be all right?" Charlie asked.

"Whatever, kid."

"Over here, then. I'll take this'un. And you can have the other." He laughed. "I was gonna offer to trade you after the first round, till I seen what you come up with. But what the hell. We're pals, right? Soon as I get done"—he patted the blonde on her ass—"I'll send her over an' we can make us that swap. I always did hear that the meat was sweetest close to the bone, eh?"

"I'll let you know later, Charlie," Raider said, although the truth was that he wanted nothing to do with the flabby whore Charlie intended to wallow in. And it was not only because he had no desire to dip his wick in Charlie Krepp's sloppy seconds.

"Okay. Whatever you say, Rade, ol' buddy." Charlie was still grinning. He led his choice quickly into the darkness of the nearest shanty. They didn't even take time to light a candle inside before Raider heard a shriek of laughter and the hearty smack of flesh on flesh. He shook his head in disbelief at the things that some people think are fun.

He had almost forgotten about the girl whose hand was nestled small and fearful in his. He looked down at her. "You okay?"

She looked at him with huge doelike eyes but did not answer. He repeated the question.

This time she did speak, but it was in a rattle of tongue-clicks and grunts that might have been a drunk with the hiccups and the urps.

That answered that, he thought. Indian, whole or half, and so fresh off the reservation that she didn't even know any English. He sure as hell could pick 'em.

"Come along, girl," he said gently and led her toward the privacy of the shack next door to Charlie's.

"We'll think o' some way to pass the time," he said.

The Indian girl silently went where he led.

CHAPTER EIGHT

Raider thumbed a matchhead aflame and applied it to the wick of a candle stuck on a nail beside the door. By the time he had done that and latched the door shut, the Indian girl had her chemise off. She stood beside the bed, still avoiding his eyes with her own.

She reminded him somehow of a bird, a very young bird, frightened and alone and fallen from its nest before it could fly.

In the chemise she had looked merely skinny and pathetic. Naked she seemed all of a piece, her body small but each part in proportion to the next. Her waist looked like a grown man ought to be able to encircle it with one hand; her breasts were small and firm, the nipples dark. For some reason, possibly cleanliness, her body had been shaved of all hair. Or maybe that was a custom of her tribe, whatever tribe that was, Raider thought. The shaven pubes gave her a childish look that was distressing until he took a closer look at her. She was young but not *that* young. Probably in her twenties.

For the first time she raised her chin enough to look him directly in the eyes. She smiled shyly and lay on the bed with her legs spread slightly apart, opening herself to him.

The bed, a cot really, with its cotton ticking mattress was

the only article of furniture in the shanty. There was the bed, the single candle, and a few pegs driven into the walls where those who were fussy about dirt on their clothing could hang their things.

Raider looked at the Indian girl and felt a swift surge of response to her naked body and willing manner. He removed his clothes and hung them on the pegs. He laid his gunbelt on the floor under the head of the cot and lay beside her.

Apparently she expected him to just jump on and start pumping, because she looked confused when he did not immediately do so.

He put an arm around her shoulders and pulled her closer. The girl snuggled against him and said something in the language he could not understand.

"Whatever," he murmured.

She said something more and ran her fingertips lightly up and down his torso, toying with the hair on his chest and teasing his nipples lightly.

"You're takin' more interest in this than I would've expected," he said. He smiled at her, and she smiled back. "Your way of sayin' thanks, I expect, because I didn't give that jehu time to put a lump on your head. Well, fair's fair. I don't mind if you want to say it this way. An' you're welcome."

She bent over him. He could smell her hair. It had no sheen to it, but it was clean. It smelled of lye soap. So did the rest of her.

She ran her tongue in circles around his nipples while her hand crept lower to fondle him and play with his balls.

"Ummm."

The girl said something, then giggled. Raider got the impression he was being complimented, although he couldn't be sure of that. For all he knew she might be cussing him in a soft voice. Even so, it sounded nice just by the way she said it.

"Yeah, that too," he said as she moved lower, leaving a thin line of moisture behind wherever her tongue roved.

She reached his shaft and licked it, cupping it carefully in the palm of one hand while she warmed his balls with the other and ran her tongue lightly up and down the length of him.

Raider shifted position to make the access easier for her, and she dipped her head to tongue his balls, too.

"Mmmm."

She smiled and took him into her mouth.

After a while he stroked the back of her head for a few moments, then lightly tugged her away from what she was doing. He was enjoying it, but there were other things to enjoy too.

She responded to his touch, once again lying on her back and opening herself for him.

Raider knelt between her thighs and sank down onto her slim body. She was so small he went about it slowly, not wanting to hurt her.

The girl reached down with both hands to find and to guide him. Her body was hot and needed no additional moisture to ease his entry.

She pulled him inside and kept her hands between them, reaching around the base of his shaft to find his balls and tease them with the fingertips of both hands while he was socketed deep inside her. The effect was more than pleasant.

"Nice," Raider said. She responded with a series of low, sharp-edged syllables.

He stroked in and out very slowly, enjoying the feel of it, until she pulled her hands away and wrapped her arms and legs tight around him.

She arched her back, straining up to meet him every time he thrust into her. She worked at it, emitting low little grunts of effort with every upward lunge of her hips and pelvis.

"Nice," he said again.

She smiled and pulled him tighter to her. Deeper into her. Small as she was, she was having no difficulty accepting him.

Raider felt the slow, fine gather of the juices deep in his balls. Felt the pressure increase and the pleasure grow. He began to pump faster and quicker, driving himself onto and into her, holding nothing back.

The girl responded, clinging to him now with arm and

leg and mouth, locked to him, pumping and bucking under him with all her strength as she sought to drain him into herself.

He exploded with a grunt of effort and stiffened as the hot, hot flow surged out of his loins and into hers.

The girl clutched at him with an almost desperate strength, molding herself to him, immobile except for a slow, soft tilting of her hips to milk the last possible drop from him.

Raider shuddered once in an aftershock of pleasure and collapsed onto her. She sighed and let her arms and the tight hold of her gripping thighs fall away from him. She seemed exhausted by the effort she had put into it.

He rolled off her and smiled, and she snuggled against him again, once more trailing her fingers lightly over his chest and belly while he relaxed and recuperated from the intensity of their coupling.

For the first time since Charlie Krepp had suggested coming here, Raider was beginning to think that the damned kid had had a pretty good idea after all.

He was in no hurry now for the second time. There was time enough and more for that. He gently stroked the back of the Indian girl's head and let his fingers trail through the cool softness of her hair.

He was in no hurry, but he certainly offered no objection when after a few short minutes the girl once again raised herself on an elbow so that she could run first the ends of her hair and then the wet heat of her tongue over his body.

He stroked her back, the skin smooth and curiously cool to the touch even though he already knew the heat that was inside that slender body, and he shifted position to encourage her when once again she moved lower with her tongue and busy, busy fingertips.

"Nice," he muttered.

The Indian girl laughed and said something in return.

Raider didn't even care that he couldn't understand what she said.

He certainly could understand what she was doing, and for the moment that was quite enough.

CHAPTER NINE

Doc was supervising the unloading of their baggage—his own Gladstone and Mrs. Boatwright's several hundred pounds of boxes, bundles, and bags—but the seemingly simple chore was becoming an embarrassment instead of a routine task.

"Be careful. Be *careful* with that, I tell you. If you scratch it, young man, I shall have you dismissed from your employment. I assure you I can do it." The lady's cultured tones had turned shrill and petulant now that she was dealing with a lowly baggage handler.

Doc suppressed his feelings on the subject while the woman was watching. As soon as she turned her head to glare at another of the Union Pacific porters and issue new instructions, he tried to take some of the sting out of her comments by winking at the kid she had been abusing.

The boy—he could not have been more than sixteen or seventeen—shrugged and winked back. Apparently he had been through this sort of thing before with persnickety passengers.

Under Weatherbee's nominal supervision and Mrs. Boatwright's constant flow of complaint, direction, and reproof, the bags eventually were transferred from the baggage car into the luggage boot of a depot hack, and Mrs. Boatwright was handed into the shaded interior of the carriage.

"Where to, bub?" the driver asked Doc.

Angela Boatwright immediately launched into a detailed list of her requirements in a hotel. The driver, a man old enough to have a beard that had lost all original color, ignored her and directed a stream of tobacco juice past the lady's open window. He looked instead at Doc and waited patiently for an address.

"The Drover's Rest," Doc said. The driver nodded, spat another stream of yellow-brown juice, and snapped his team into motion.

Mrs. Boatwright looked miffed. "This Drover's Rest, is it suitable? Are the accommodations the best that are available in Ogallala?"

"Yes," Doc lied. Actually there was another hotel, much smaller and much more expensive, that would have offered better rooms. But if John Boatwright or any of his crew had gotten as far as Ogallala they would almost certainly have stopped at the Drover's Rest, which catered to the tastes of the cattlemen who were beginning to stream into western Nebraska as the ponderous herds filled up the empty grasslands of the Sand Hills.

And if any member of the crew had survived to reach the town, the Drover's Rest was the most likely place for Doc to learn about it. He intended to stay there regardless of Mrs. Boatwright's wishes. Besides, the train ride from Kansas City had already convinced him that the woman would not be satisfied regardless of what she was given, so there seemed no point in worrying about it.

The woman sniffed, her nose stuck high in the air, and muttered something. Doc could not make out what she had said, but the tone of it was dire.

He reached for a cheroot, and Mrs. Boatwright made a face. "Please. I have *asked* you not to smoke those horrid things in my presence."

It was Doc's turn to mutter something. But he put the cigar away.

The Drover's Rest was only a few blocks away from the

railroad depot, close to the complex maze of stock pens where beeves were loaded for shipment east and where other herds of breeding animals were unloaded for trailing to the rich grass country around the booming town. The hack driver had them there within minutes, and a laconic, sleepy-eyed porter appeared with a hand truck to take charge of the baggage. Doc hustled Mrs. Boatwright inside before she had time to get them off on the wrong foot with the Drover's Rest employees.

His effort had been in vain, though. No sooner had Mrs. Boatwright reached the registration desk than her nose went into the air again and she began making her demands known.

"Your best suite," she said. "Your very best, mind now. And a room for my man here."

Her *man?* Doc's stomach churned. Her *man?* There were a great many things he was willing to do for Allan Pinkerton, but becoming some high and mighty bitch's *man* was not among them.

Still, he managed to keep his mouth shut, even though he was seething under the surface.

"No suites," the desk man said.

The fellow was dressed in sleeve garters and a green visor, but no amount of exterior trappings could make him look like anything but what he was—and that was a leather-faced, sun-dried cowhand who could no longer handle the rough string. He had a twisted leg and a stiff hip and might have been working indoors for years, but his hands still looked like they belonged around a rope instead of the steel-nibbed pen he was holding.

"What?" Mrs. Boatwright sounded like she was sure she had misunderstood. Her nose went another notch or two higher.

"No suites, lady. We got rooms. You want a room or not?"

She sniffed. "Have you, then, a proper room? A decent room?"

"Shit, yes," the broken-down cowhand drawled. "They got solid walls, doors, all that crap. You want a room?"

Angela Boatwright looked uncertainly toward Doc. It was, he thought, the first time she had been uncertain about *any*thing since he had met her.

"Two rooms," Doc said.

"Adjoinin'?"

"Not particularly."

The clerk chuckled and assigned them rooms on different floors.

"I don't like that man's manner," Mrs. Boatwright complained loudly as Doc took her by the elbow and steered her up the stairs toward her room. The clerk had absolutely assured her that it was the very, *very* best the Drover's Rest had to offer. It also happened to be on the top floor of the hotel. And Doc happened to have stayed here several times in the past. Enough to know that each and every room in the place was identical to all the others. Mrs. Angela Boatwright was going to be getting her exercise. And likely the one-time cowboy would get a chuckle out of it every time she puffed her way up those stairs. Doc kept his face straight and escorted her to her room.

"The bath," she said when she was shown inside. "Where is the bath?"

The bellman who had guided them was another former cowhand. He was not so visibly crippled as the man at the desk, although he was missing several fingers from his right hand. A dally roper, then, not one of the south country tie-fast ropers, because it was the dally ropers who tended to lose fingers when a coil slipped. And to have been in the business long enough to get the gray in his hair he likely had come out of Oregon, Doc concluded.

The bellman pointed toward a door at the end of the public hallway. "Ten cents extra for fresh water," he said. "No charge to use whatever's already settin' in the tub." He grinned, exposing a line of pink gun and one lonely, yellow tooth.

Angela Boatwright puffed up like she was ready to explode. Before she could do so Doc tipped the bellman and hustled him out the door—although the fellow acted like he would have enjoyed staying and watching the explosion.

Obviously it had not taken long for word about this newly registered guest to get around to the staff.

"What about my bags?" Mrs. Boatwright shrilled as the bellman disappeared down the hall. "Where are my *bags?*"

"They'll be along direc'ly," the bellman floated over his shoulder.

"But . . ."

"It's all right," Doc assured her. "After all, you have to expect rather, uh, primitive conditions in a cow town." He smiled disarmingly.

"But my things. I have to bathe after that horrid train ride." Doc had found the trip to be remarkably comfortable. "All that soot," she pouted. "I simply must change. And the bank. We must get to the bank before it closes. And this room." She turned to survey the place and wrinkled her nose. "It is wretched."

Doc shrugged. "It's the best they have. The clerk told you that."

"But how shall I call for my bath water? There is no pull, no speaking tube."

Doc shrugged again. "I expect you'll have to tell them at the desk."

"That is four floors *down,*" she wailed. "And four flights back up again."

"You did say you wanted the best."

She looked as though she didn't know whether to scream or to cry. Her eyes narrowed, and she peered at Doc. She could see no traces of sympathy there and apparently decided that neither would do any good.

"You may leave me now," she said. She had been off balance for only a moment or two there. The bitchiness was back in her tone of voice.

Doc bowed slightly in her direction and let himself out the door. He was able to keep the amusement off his face until the room door was shut behind him and he was out in the empty hallway.

He went down to his own second-floor room, convenient to the stairs leading down to the bar and the restaurant that was attached to the hotel, and found his Gladstone already there, a pitcher of fresh water on his washstand, and fluffy, clean-smelling towels laid out ready for his use.

He grinned as he washed up. These old boys at the Drover's Rest might be a bunch of has-been hicks, but they knew how to run a nice place when they wanted to.

CHAPTER TEN

The president of the Stockmen's Bank of Commerce was nearly as pompous as Angela Boatwright was bitchy. The man's name was G. Horace Markley. Doc was sure of this because the name was displayed in gilt lettering on the front window glass, on the door to his private office, *and* on a plaque that sat on his desk. G. Horace Markley was taking no chances that someone might remain ignorant about who the big cheese was in this bank.

"I really haven't time for this," Markley said. He had already looked at his watch twice since they were allowed into the office. "I already responded to your telegraphed inquiry, Mrs. Boatwright. I expected to see your husband. Arrangements had been made. By a, uh . . . oh, whatever his name was. Some fellow in Shreveport."

"Pinchot," Mrs. Boatwright injected. "Jean-Louis Pinchot." The chin hiked upward. *"Colonel* Pinchot, if you please, sir."

"Yes, whatever," Markley said, dismissing the down-south banker with a wave of his hand. "Anyway, the arrangements had been made. We were fully prepared to accept Mr., uh, Boatwright's deposit and, uh, to accommodate this Pinchot person with a letter of credit and transfer of funds. The gentleman in question, however, failed to arrive here. No deposit was ever made. Therefore no letter of credit was ever extended. And that, I assure you, is the extent of my knowledge on the subject."

"Have you proof of that, sir?" Mrs. Boatwright demanded coldly. She sounded like she was talking to the baggage porter at the railroad depot.

Markley gave her a look that was even colder than the ones she was giving him. "One gives proofs of deposits made, madam. Not of intentions unmet."

"I don't think this is getting us anywhere," Doc said. "Besides, Mrs. Boatwright, Mr. Markley's reputation in banking circles is unmatched for his integrity and acumen."

Markley beamed as he nodded with a display of assumed humility.

Actually Doc had no idea in the world what G. Horace Markley's reputation was. For all he knew the man might be a shyster of the first water.

That was, however, unlikely. In a location like this one, cattle, the buying and selling and financing of them, would be Markley's stock in trade. And cattlemen are a gossipy, clannish crowd. If one of them got a raw deal, all of them would know it. And Markley's business would wither away to nothing virtually overnight—which G. Horace Markley would comprehend as quickly as anyone.

Still, there were no guarantees. A quarter of a million dollars in clear and sudden profit would be enough to tempt anyone. And to sway a healthy percentage of those who were tempted. Markley might well have succumbed to the lures of free and easy money.

From Doc Weatherbee's point of view, though, the *last* person to ask about that would be G. Horace Markley. Other avenues of inquiry would quite certainly be better onces than this pointless confrontation in Markley's office.

So at the moment Doc was more interested in smoothing ruffled feathers than in gathering information.

He got both parties calm and escorted Mrs. Boatwright out into the bright sunshine of the streets of Ogallala.

"The gentleman is really that reputable?" the woman asked as they walked back toward the hotel.

Doc shrugged. "Darned if I know, to tell you the truth. But I'll find out."

She gave him a questioning look and seemed close to anger once again.

"Probably he's telling the truth," Doc said. "I spent considerable time last night trying to find out if anyone in town remembers seeing your husband or any member of his crew. They didn't check in to the Drover's Rest, and no one else I've talked to has seen them. If anyone had, well, then would be the time to get suspicious of Mr. Markley and his bank. Your husband might have gone straight to the bank when they hit town, you see, but the rest of those boys wouldn't. They'd have headed for the saloons or the hotel or for sure the barbershop. Which reminds me, I need to stop over there and ask of the barber. He was closed when I went by there last night."

"But you do intend to inquire about that wretched Markley person also?"

"Sure." Doc nodded. "But it isn't high on my list of priorities because, as I said, there's no indication your husband ever got this far with his crew and that rather large amount of currency. So what I'll do will be to send off a few telegrams to Chicago. The home office can check on Markley there much better than I can here, anyway."

"I don't understand," Angela Boatwright admitted.

Doc smiled and explained. "In town here, folks will mostly know the front Markley gives them to see. But back in Chicago is where all the big stockyard buyers are headquartered—there or in Kansas City—and the Pinkerton Agency has excellent contacts in both places. Not only with the major buyers, you see, but with the insurance companies, courier and transport services, all the agencies and companies that service the banking business. The Pinkerton Agency happens to service those same firms which service the banks in one capacity or another. So a single wire sent to our home office will provide more real information about Markley and his bank than a whole week of inquiries here in Ogallala."

"I see," she said. She looked thoughtful. "You and your,

uh, partner, then, are more than mere muscular gunmen?"

Doc was too amused by the remark to feel insulted by it. He threw his head back and laughed. "Mrs. Boatwright, I rarely even carry a firearm."

She smiled. "But you are rather muscular, aren't you?"

Doc escorted her back into the hotel and up all the flights of stairs to her room. It occurred to him that the prongs of the desk clerk's little joke were gouging more than just Angela Boatwright.

She handed him her room key so he could unlock the door and open it for her. When he tried to return the room key to her she ignored it and whisked on inside, obviously expecting him to follow. He did, reluctantly.

Once the door was shut behind them, Angela Boatwright dropped her chin and smiled at him shyly past lowered eyelids. Slowly and quite deliberately she licked her full, red lips.

Doc felt a stirring of desire. He did not want it, but it was undeniably there.

The woman was a bitch. She had demonstrated that almost continuously since they left Kansas City.

Yet she was a damned beauty, too. Her face. Her figure. When she chose to, she could make a man's mouth water.

When she chose to, Doc reminded himself.

At other times, most times, she was demanding, demeaning, imperious, cold. That was the norm for her. This was the first time he had seen this side of her. Yet even knowing all he did about her, he couldn't help but respond to the raw, superheated sensuality that flowed out of her eyes and seemed to charge the air between them.

There was something else, Doc reminded himself. Whatever had happened that night she had spent with Rade— and likely he would never know what that had been—Raider had not been happy about it in the morning.

Whatever it had been, Doc didn't want now to experience it in Raider's place.

Yet there was clear invitation in the look she was giving him.

There was an open sexuality in her eyes and in the cant

of her shoulders, the provocative jutting thrust of her bosom. It was as if all of a sudden she had begun to give off a musky scent of lust. The change in her was extraordinary. And truly unwanted.

Doc reached behind him, fumbling for the doorknob.

His intentions were firm. He should turn and get the hell out of here. Now.

But . . .

Angela took a step forward, and then another. She reached up to touch his jaw. Even that small contact was searing, electric. He jumped.

Angela laughed, a low furry sound that rumbled up from deep in her throat.

"I'm not always disagreeable, dear man," she whispered.

Some remote, detached part of his mind registered the fact that she knew, then, how unpleasant she could be. She did it deliberately, which was perhaps even worse than the kind of person who is unknowingly boorish.

But that part of Doc's thinking was very far away from the reality of the effect she was having on him.

The look she had given him, the so brief touch of her fingertips to his jaw, had him achingly erect. The front of his carefully tailored trousers bulged at an angle no tailor would ever have condoned.

Angela pressed closer to him. Her hand left his jaw to lend its heat to the rise behind his fly. She chuckled again and raised her lips to his, molding her lush body against his and sucking his tongue into her mouth.

Doc knew he ought to resist her. He truly wanted to. But even while he was thinking that, Angela was loosening his tie, undoing the buttons on his shirt, running the palm of one hand over his chest while with the other she unfastened the buttons of his fly.

By then it was too late.

She drew him toward the bed, discarding her own clothing as she went.

She did it with too much ease, Doc thought. With too much practice. He felt sorry for John Boatwright, a man he had never met and probably never would. Anyone who was married to a woman like this would have nothing but trouble. But anyone who bedded her . . .

Angela sat on the edge of the bed and pulled the last of Doc's clothing from him. She threw the cloth aside and cupped him in her hands. She bent forward.

She engulfed him. Not slowly but with a furious greed. Tongue, lips, hands, throat, all pulling at him. Surrounding him. So hot. So very good.

He could not remember anything that had ever been so hot or so pleasant.

But then, at the moment he was not interested in trying to remember or to think about anything at all.

It didn't last nearly long enough. Seconds, minutes, he couldn't be sure. What he knew for certain was that he wanted it to continue. He didn't want this sensation to stop. He would have resented even a climax because that would have made it end.

But it did end. Abruptly, without warning.

Angela pulled back away from him, leaving behind only a searing memory of overloaded nerve endings.

She chuckled and tugged him down beside the bed until he was kneeling between her spread, velvet thighs.

"Do me," she commanded.

She arched her hips upward, straining toward him. The hairs of her dark bush were trimmed and neat. A scented powder had been applied there. The lips of her sex gaped wide and wet in front of him. Pink and glistening with her juices. Sweet smelling and desirable.

"Do me," she snapped. "Now!" She grabbed at him. "Right *now.*"

The selfishly haughty demand snapped Doc back to reality.

This woman was beautiful. All ripe curves and heated passions.

But she was a bitch. She wanted to take. She cared nothing about giving. Anything she gave would be grudgingly offered, a bribe, nothing more than a tool she could use to take control so that her own desires might be met.

There would be no shared pleasures with this one, no mutual satisfaction.

Doc shook his head. A shudder ran up and down the length of his spine. He had a remote, distant feeling, as if he was just wakening from a bad dream.

He could still recall with complete clarity the feel of her. The heat and the moisture and the total sensations as she engulfed his shaft totally.

But it was only a memory of that dream, and he was awake again now.

He grinned and stood, naked, towering over her.

"Do me," she shrieked. Her face contorted with sudden rage, twisting her features and making them ugly. "You bastard. Now."

Doc's desire for her faded as quickly as it had come, evaporating away until there was nothing left. Instead he felt only sadness for her, for all the things she would never understand and all the joys she would forever be unable to share.

He wondered if it would do any good if he sat on the bed beside her. Petted and comforted her. Tried to explain to her the way it could be between a man and a woman.

Angela answered that question for him. Her face still disfigured by fury, she came surging off the bed with her fingers curved talonlike, her nails clawing. She cursed him, using words he would not have suspected she would even know, taunting him for a lack of manhood. Yet still demanding that he allow himself to be used as a tool to satisfy her lusts.

"Thank you," Doc said gently. He evaded a rake of her nails and reached for his clothes.

"Don't you mock me, you useless son of a bi—"

"I'm not mocking you," he said in a soft voice. "You've given me a lesson, and I thank you for that."

"What the fuck?"

He smiled at her. "You've been teaching me about compassion. Understanding. Empathy, really. You help me to understand how a whore must feel or the way it must have been for a slave with a demanding master. So I meant that. Thank you."

"You son of a bitch."

Doc shrugged and went on dressing. He pulled his coat on and picked up his spats and tie. At least she was no longer trying to scratch his eyes out. He appreciated the improvement.

"If you ever want to try lovemaking instead of fucking, you know . . ." He smiled. "Or maybe you don't. It's what people do *with* one another instead of *to* someone else. Well, if you do, look me up. I think you could be a nice person if you wanted to."

Angela Boatwright worked up a mouthful of spittle and spat at him. She missed.

Doc smiled at her. He put his curled-brim derby on and let himself out of her hotel room.

Her curses reached him through the closed door until he was halfway down the hall to the stairs.

CHAPTER ELEVEN

"That's the place," Charlie Krepp said, pointing.

Raider pulled his horse to a halt and leaned back against his cantle. He hooked a knee over his horn and sat there for a few minutes to get a good look at the Timmons ranch headquarters before they rode on down.

The outfit was set against the south side of a low hill where at least some of the icy north winds of winter would be broken. West of the headquarters there was a stand of runty cedar or some similar growth with a few pale-leafed low trees mixed in.

"There's a spring over in the trees," Charlie volunteered.

Raider grunted and continued his inspection. The place had been there for some time, as evidenced by the weathered poles of the corrals and the obvious age of the stone house, bunkhouse, and other outbuildings.

There was a good deal of upgrading going on now, though. The corrals had been expanded to roughly three times their original size, the new enclosures built from freshly peeled poles that stood out a bright yellow in contrast to the pale gray of the older pens.

And there was a crew of workmen swarming at the east end of the Timmons home, building a wing that would more than double the size of the original house. The old structure had been built with native stone. The new wing was of brick. Freight costs alone to get all that brick down here would be fierce, Raider thought.

"Looks like Timmons is doing himself pretty proud," Raider said.

"Them boys ain't wasting any time about it, neither," Charlie said. "When we was here before they barely had the foundations started. Now the walls is half up."

Raider grunted and returned to a proper seat in his saddle. "Let's go down and pay them a call."

They dropped down off the hill that sheltered the head-quarters buildings and rode into the ranch yard. The work-men at the far end of the house ignored them, but after a moment the front door banged open and a young woman in a yellow dress came out onto the porch.

"That's old man Timmons's daughter," Charlie whis-pered. "Name's Miss Crystal." He grinned. "Ain't she somethin'?"

Raider got a better look as they came closer to the house. Given Charlie's tastes in women he could see the attraction. Timmons's daughter had tits enough for herself and three sisters. Apart from that, though, the girl was plain, with mouse-colored hair pulled back in a severe bun, gold wire spectacles, and thin, dry lips. Raider marveled anew at Charlie Krepp's lack of discrimination about what rattled his chain.

"My father is not hiring . . . oh, it's you," she said as they reached the porch and stopped the horses.

"Yes'm," Charlie said. He grinned sheepishly and re-moved his hat, holding it against his chest and blushing so hard his freckles nearly disappeared.

"Mr. Krepp, I already told you—"

"Yes, Miss Crystal, I know that, but I come here with my good friend Raider here." Charlie grinned even wider. "My pal Rade is a Pinkerton man, Miss Crystal. And maybe the best hand with a gun there's ever been. We came up here lookin' into the disappearance of John Boatwright, what your daddy bought those cows from." He managed to sound self-important and very much a part of the investigation.

"Oh." The girl shifted her attention to Raider. She pushed her spectacles higher on the bridge of her nose and gave him a closer look. "I see."

"We would like to see your father if it's convenient, Miss Timmons," Raider said politely.

"You'll have to wait, then," she said. "My father is away for a few days." She shrugged. "Doing something with those cows, but I don't know what."

Raider nodded. Nine thousand head of newly delivered cattle would have to be separated into smaller herds for grazing management and distributed over whatever territory Timmons controlled. It was understandable that the boss and his men would need some time to get the job done. On the other hand, Raider didn't want to waste time here sitting on his butt if he didn't have to.

"Would you know where they could be located, Miss Timmons?"

She shook her head. "They could be anywhere. In any direction at all. I wouldn't have any idea how to find them. But he said he would be back the day after tomorrow at the latest. He could come home this evening instead for all I know. The bunkhouse is empty while everyone is out, so you can put your things in there. I'd offer you a place in the house, but we haven't room for guests quite yet."

"No need for that, miss, but we thank you." Raider deliberately said "we" even though the apologetic not-quite-invitation had obviously been directed toward him and not Charlie. Raider suspected that Charlie had made some advances toward the girl when he was here last, and those advances had not been well received.

"You must, of course, take dinner with us," Crystal Timmons added. "We have more than enough room at the table. And our regular cook is out with the riding crew."

Raider glanced toward the workmen who were busy just past the end of the porch.

"They fix for themselves," the girl explained.

"Well, thank you for the hospitality, then," Raider said.

"You are quite welcome, sir." She smiled. "Supper will be just after dark."

"We'll be on time," Raider promised. He touched the brim of his Stetson and wheeled his horse toward the low-roofed bunkhouse. Charlie trailed along behind him.

They dismounted, and Charlie jumped forward to take Raider's reins. "I'll tend to the horse, Rade. You go ahead an' get comfortable."

"I'd be a lot more comfortable if we could get down to business here instead of waiting around for the man of the house."

"Well, me, I don't mind a little wait," Charlie said. "Not if it means I can have some words with Miss Crystal. She sure is a looker, ain't she?"

"Outstanding," Raider agreed, although he did not think Charlie was referring to the girl's looks any more than Raider was. She had only one asset—well, two—but that was as far as that went.

Charlie led the horses away toward the corrals, and Raider went inside to find an empty bunk.

Raider shook his head vigorously in refusal of a third slice of the pie Mrs. Timmons was trying to press on him. "Thank you, ma'am, but I'm groaning already. I just couldn't."

"If you are sure?" she asked.

"Positive, ma'am, thank you. And we do thank you for such a fine meal. I haven't enjoyed anything so much in ever so long."

The woman beamed with pleasure. She was a plump, matronly woman of middle years who probably had looked very much the same as her daughter when she was young. By now, though, her figure had collapsed into a suety lump. She seemed nice enough, though, Raider thought, and she sure could handle a stove and ladle.

"This is an awfully nice place you have here, ma'am," Raider observed. "Have you been here long?"

"No, just since last fall. Maxwell, that's my husband,

Maxwell Timmons, you see, brought us here then. From Wisconsin. Do you know that part of the country, Mr. Raider?"

"Not very well, ma'am," Raider said. "Only to pass through."

"It really is quite lovely," Mrs. Timmons said. Raider thought he could detect a note of wistfulness in the woman's voice. She missed the home they had left behind.

Wisconsin was not exactly ranch country, though. He wondered what had brought them west. And how they had managed to come with enough cash to get into ranching on such an extremely large scale. That was not the sort of thing he could directly ask, but there was nothing to stop him from tickling the edges of it.

"You must have quite a spread here," he prompted.

"Oh my, yes." Mrs. Timmons laughed. "Back home we had ten acres. Out here I don't know how many *sections* we have. A section, you know, is a whole mile square. Maxwell taught me that. But I don't think *he* knows how many sections we control now."

"Really?"

"Oh, yes. I can't begin to comprehend it all. There is this place, of course. Which we bought from a Mr. Stuart. Part of that we own outright, land Mr. Stuart and some of his men had homesteaded, but that has something to do with owning just the water so that you control the grass around it. I'm not sure just how that works, although Maxwell has tried to explain it to me ever so many times. And then there is some more land we bought from the government. And leases—from the government some of them, and from the Indian reservation, and . . . I simply don't know what all else. It is all so confusing."

"Yes, ma'am."

Raider reached for a toothpick from the little dish of them provided in the center of the table. Across from him, Charlie was leaning to the side and whispering something to Crystal Timmons, who was doing her best to ignore him.

Bought an established, operating ranch, Raider was thinking. Bought more land and leased other pieces. Bought nine thousand head of stockers. For cash. That he knew about.

A deal like that would take money by the damn carload. There wouldn't be any one bank in Montana big enough to hold it all.

He took another look at Mrs. Timmons, smiling at her and patting his overfull stomach to hide what he was thinking, and wondered about that.

Neither Timmons's wife nor his daughter looked like the kind who had all that kind of money behind them.

Angela Boatwright, now, no one would think twice if she showed up flashing a bank account that would choke a mule. Hell, from her you expected it.

But these two?

He looked from the mother to the daughter and back again.

Both of them were wearing plain, cheap dresses that they might have made themselves. For sure it wasn't any fancy custom seamstress who had put those dresses together.

And neither one of them wore a lick of jewelry, except for a wire-thin and severely plain wedding band on Mrs. Timmons's plump ring finger. The gold band looked like it would have cost two dollars from any crossroads general store. And it wasn't new, either. It had been bought and put onto her when she was a sight slimmer than she was now, and the band of gold cut deep into the flesh on that finger. It looked like it ought to hurt like hell, although she seemed unaware of it.

Raider grunted softly to himself, trying to tote up in his mind all the ways money was being flung to the winds here.

Land. Cattle. Improvements to the place. And not cheap ones, either. The brickwork going into the house expansion alone would beggar an ordinary man.

Raider decided there was a great deal more he needed to learn about this Maxwell Timmons.

This was the last place John Boatwright had been seen alive, after all.

And come to think of it, Charlie Krepp said Boatwright was paid off in $240,000 in currency. Paper money was out of the ordinary in this country anyway, where men tended to trust hard money only and where most would not work for anyone who paid in paper.

And one of the reasons men tended to distrust currency was that it was so easily faked. A banker might be able to spot the difference immediately, but the average man out here saw paper currency so rarely that he would not be expected to detect counterfeits.

Raider chewed on that thought as slowly as he had chewed on those last bites of pie.

Just suppose, he thought, Timmons paid Boatwright off in funny money. Then suppose he knew he would have to do something, like when Boatwright was not expecting it, to recover that funny money and keep John Boatwright from exposing him.

It would be an easy enough sort of thing to arrange, Raider concluded. He could tell Boatwright that he had gotten a loan at the bank, then pay off with worthless paper instead of real currency.

The cattle would be delivered and bills of sale signed— that would have been a necessary step for the swindle to work, Raider realized, because the Montana stock inspectors were a sharp crowd and noted for their honesty—then everything would have been all good cheer and fellowship.

And it would not be unreasonable of Timmons and his crew at the last minute to ask Boatwright and his men to help them sort the herd or advise on how the smaller, split-off herds should be grouped. After all, this crowd from east Texas had spent a lot of time trailing the nine thousand beeves across country. It would be only natural that their advice might be sought on how to handle the animals after they were delivered.

Raider sucked on the toothpick and reflected on how very easy it would be for Timmons's crew to lull Boatwright and his men into a position where they could all be put under the gun at once. Or separated and taken one or two at a time, for that matter.

Then the counterfeit money could be recovered and burned, and any stray bodies disposed of.

Sure, Raider thought, it would be easy.

And in effect, Maxwell Timmons would end up with nine thousand head of good breeding stock—plenty of animals to mortgage for real cash when he needed some—at no more cost than that of a few boxes of cartridges.

It was damned well something to consider, Raider told himself. And something to look into.

That much currency, if real, would have had to have come from somewhere traceable, Raider thought. There would not be so many banks in the country capable of handling a cash delivery of that amount, either. It should be no trick to check up on them.

He made a mental note to do that, first chance he got.

"Ma'am?" He was jarred out of his thoughts by a realization that Mrs. Timmons had been saying something. He smiled at her. "Sorry. Reckon I was wool-gathering."

"I asked if you would like another cup of coffee?"

"Why, yes, ma'am, that would be nice. Thank you."

She gave him a wide, motherly smile and went to the kitchen to fetch the coffeepot.

CHAPTER TWELVE

Angela Boatwright gave Doc a cold look. Well, that was nothing new. She had given him nothing but cold looks ever since he had called at her room this morning before breakfast. And she had not spoken to him yet.

Still, the fact that she was not even going to complain about the transportation he had arranged was an ominous sign indeed. Mrs. Boatwright had never yet been slow to complain about anything. And after last night Doc had expected a real storm when she got a look at the rickety spring wagon that was the only vehicle he had been able to find for a long-term rental. A barouche and four would not have pleased her, of course. He knew that. But a spring wagon would positively insult her. Yet still she said nothing.

She did not even speak when the innocent-faced but devilish-eyed hotel porter threw her luggage negligently into the back of the wagon, wiped his hands, spat, and sauntered away without waiting for a tip. Doc gathered that the staff of the Drover's Rest was glad to get rid of her.

Doc helped her into the driving box of the old rig, then walked around to the other side and climbed up beside her. The seat was not exactly what he would call comfortable. At some time in the distant past someone had tried to pad the wooden planks with an application of old rags, but time and use had taken their toll. About the only thing left of the padding was a few scraps of cloth stuck to the tack heads that protruded from the seat, lying in wait there to snag passengers' clothing. Doc was glad he had switched to trousers suitable for rough travel. Mrs. Boatwright was still turned out for city living.

He took up the reins of the mismatched pair of cobs that had come with the rig and chatted to her just as if everything was normal between them.

"Absolutely no sign of your husband or any of the crew here," he said. "I've asked everyplace I could think of in town, but no one remembers seeing them. That isn't a guarantee, of course, because a great many strangers pass through Ogallala. But there is no indication they ever reached the town. And I checked the public barns, also. No sign of their horses either. That is one of the things you want to look for, of course. Sometimes it's easier to make a person disappear than the horse he has been riding." He reached for a cheroot. Mrs. Boatwright might well object, but they were in the open air. The hell with her. He pulled it out and lighted it.

Still no complaints. Darned if he wasn't beginning to like this sulky side of her.

"I sent those wires too, of course. The ones we discussed yesterday, if you recall. If there is anything we need to know about the friendly local banker, Chicago will find out and report to us. Although frankly I would not expect anything there. Not without some independent observation that your husband ever reached Ogallala. No, I think they were stopped somewhere north of here. Quite possibly at or near the ranch where the herd was delivered."

The wagon was reaching the end of the more or less maintained stretches of public road in Ogallala and heading out of town on a primitive track to the north. The jolting and jostling was becoming constant. Still there were no complaints.

Doc decided it was time to throw in a question. Just to see if she would answer. Although if this sullen silence was her idea of punishment, she was going to be disappointed.

Doc enjoyed his own company entirely too much for solitude or silence to bother him.

"That really was quite a herd," he ventured. "Not many men can put up that large a traveling herd from their own stock. Why did John agree to sell so many? Do you know?"

Angela stared straight ahead. Her chin was held high and her jaw set, and her eyes never strayed from the road ahead of them.

She had her feet braced against the mudboard at the front of the wagon and was gripping the edge of the seat with both hands. Even so, the rocking and bouncing of the wagon were causing her to sway and shift constantly.

Doc glanced down. Her knuckles were white where she was clinging to the seat front, trying to maintain her balance and keep from bumping into Doc's shoulder just a few inches from hers.

He smiled to himself. If she was going to keep that up for the whole day's travel she was going to be one weary female by the end of the day.

A mad one, too. Already he could see some strands of pale blue thread stuck on the tack heads on the seat. Angela Boatwright's gown today was pale blue. He suspected this would be the last wearing she got out of the garment.

"We won't bother to stop at every ranch we see," he went on just as if they were talking. "I believe that would be a waste of time so close to Ogallala. I'm told the next town is Beam's Crossing. There's a ferry there where we can cross the North Platte. We should reach it by late afternoon."

Angela Boatwright's expression became even more bleak than it already was, presumably at the prospect of spending so many hours in the bouncing wagon. But still she said nothing.

"I had the hotel pack a box lunch for us," he said pleasantly. "Liverwurst sandwiches and cold chicken. I hope that meets your approval."

Angela gritted her teeth and stared down the road beyond the ears of the patient, plodding horses.

CHAPTER THIRTEEN

Raider wished Maxwell Timmons would get the hell home. The man's women were about to drive him around the bend.

Crystal was openly making calf's eyes at him. And her mother was encouraging it. For some reason the fool woman had decided she should take Raider to raise. At least that was the only way he could figure it, the way she was always mothering him and pushing choice bits of food at him during the meals and wanting to wash out his clothes and such. And the way she kept telling him how Crystal had cooked this or Crystal could mend that or Crystal had done thus-and-such. Lordy but he was commencing to feel over-whelmed.

Obvious about it? Shit, he reckoned they were.

Meanwhile Charlie Krepp was as happy as a hog in a mire. Charlie seemed oblivious to the whole performance by the Timmons women and more than once confided in his great and good pal Raider that he, Charlie, was going to make Miss Crystal his wife.

Good luck to him, was Raider's opinion. He would be happy if the girl *and* her damned mother would put their sights on Charlie instead of him.

Come to think of it, Charlie was beginning to drag on him too, Raider thought.

Right now the kid had given up questioning Raider about the intricacies of six-gun handling—although *that* respite would only be temporary, Raider was sure—and now he was sitting on his bunk with a dull pocketknife trying to whittle his cast-off army issue holster into something better than a deep pouch that a revolver could be stored in.

Raider had spent the better part of the day out around the sheds and corrals trying to find something that needed fixing. But Timmons's damned work crew already had every fence so tight and every gate so true that there wasn't shit Raider could find to occupy himself with. And waiting was not something he did either cheerfully or well.

No help for it, though. He had already tried talking to the workmen who were still scurrying like so many ants around the rising walls of the house addition. The men were mostly Scandanavians whose English was sketchy even on those rare occasions when their accents could be fathomed.

The job foreman spoke the least English of any of them, so he was no help. Mrs. Timmons had explained right proudly that her husband could make out in Norwegian, so he didn't have any problem talking with his workmen.

She had volunteered that after she saw Raider trying to talk with the men. He rather seriously doubted that she knew Raider's interest in conversation with him had nothing to do with comments about the admittedly excellent work they were doing. Instead he was looking for information from them that might trip up Maxwell Timmons and put the SOB in jail for murder.

Raider sighed. And *that* was all still supposition too. His theories about the counterfeiting were a long way from being proved out. First he needed to meet this Timmons and have some checking done on the man's background. And, truthfully, he wanted to talk to Weatherbee about it too.

There were times when the old son of a bitch was a pain. But Doc had a pretty fair head on his shoulders when it came to a job, and this was one Raider wanted to try out on Doc before he took it any further. He damn sure couldn't talk to Charlie Krepp about it.

He looked across the room at Charlie. The kid finished

taking another slice of leather off his holster so that the trigger guard of the ancient Colt would be exposed. He admired the modification with a grin and tossed the scrap of old leather into a corner, where it joined an accumulation of litter that must have taken the ranch hands years to assemble.

"What d'you think, Rade?"

"Uh huh," Raider said. He hoped that would be taken as a compliment of sorts, because he didn't want to hurt the kid's feelings. But damned if he was going to lie to him either.

They heard the dinner bell ring over at the main house, and Charlie jumped to his feet, still with that grin on his face. "C'mon, Rade. Supper's ready."

"Okay." Raider was not so eager. Charlie seemed to have a stomach that was bottomless, but Raider felt like he had done nothing but eat ever since he got here. And Mrs. Timmons did not make it any easier by pushing all that stuff on him. Even at that it wouldn't have been so bad except that the damned woman was such a *good* cook. Raider was enjoying it in spite of himself. And *that* pissed him off.

They ate hugely once again, and after dinner Mrs. Timmons asked Raider if he would remain behind for a little while. There was something she wanted to discuss with him.

"Yes, ma'am."

Charlie looked like he didn't want to be left out of whatever it was, but the request had rather pointedly been made only to Raider so he had no choice but to excuse himself and go back to the bunkhouse alone.

"Yes, ma'am?" Raider asked when Charlie was gone. Crystal had left the room too, disappearing somewhere in the back of the house.

Mrs. Timmons patted Raider's cheek. "Wait in the parlor if you would, please." She smiled. "Better yet, you can sit in Maxwell's study. It's more private there."

"Yes, ma'am."

Raider went into the study and left the door open behind him. He had not been in the room before. Its furnishings were the very model of what a cattleman's office/study should

be, from the rolltop desk to the glass-fronted gun cabinet
to the mule deer and elk racks mounted on the walls. Raider
knew good and well that Maxwell Timmons had not been
here long enough to have shot those heads himself, so they
probably had been left behind by the former owner of the
place. That idea did nothing to improve Raider's opinion of
Timmons, a man he had yet to meet, because he was always
damned well suspicious of any man who would hang another
man's kill on his walls. Still, the place was nicely appointed
and comfortable.

He lighted a wall lamp near the door and helped himself
to a glass of liquor from an unlabeled decanter on a heavy
sideboard. He had no idea what the stuff was, but it was
damn sure smooth. He settled into an overstuffed leather
armchair that faced the fireplace in the front wall of the
room and took another swallow of the excellent liquor.

Raider's gun came into his hand without conscious
thought. Someone had slipped into the room behind him.
Very quietly. He had not heard the person approach.

The first he knew anyone was there was when he heard
the door latch close, and then almost immediately the lamp
was blown out.

The room was in total darkness. There was a faint sound
of breathing so he knew he was not alone.

Raider thumbed back the hammer of the Remington and
aimed the revolver toward the faintly heard sounds.

"Oh!" The voice was more gasp than word. The sound
of the hammer being cocked had been recognized.

The sound was also made by a woman.

Women could kill too, though. Raider kept his Remington cocked and aimed. He didn't know what the hell was
up here, but he wasn't going to take any chances about it.
It was always possible that Timmons had gotten word about
the visit of a Pinkerton operative and asked his womenfolk
to dispose of the problem for him. Raider had heard of
stranger things in his time.

"Where . . . where are you?" It was Crystal's voice.

Raider hesitated.

"Raider? Honey?" Definitely Crystal's voice.

"Here," he said softly. The thickly padded back of the chair was between him and the door. If there were any surprises . . .

There was no blast of gunfire in the darkness. "Would you . . . put that pistol away? Please?"

"Show yourself first, Crystal."

"Just a minute."

He could hear the faint sound of feet—bare feet?—moving on the hardwood floor, then a thin rattle of some kind, finally the scrape of a match head.

The match flared bright in the intense dark.

Crystal was not armed. Her hands were empty except for the match she held out in front of her.

She was not carrying any concealed weapons. Raider was sure of that, stone positive, because she had nowhere to conceal a weapon.

The girl was bare-assed naked.

Raider uncocked the Remington and slid it back into his holster. Crystal blew out the match.

She came toward him, feeling her way past the furniture. She found him with a light, tentative touch on the sleeve, then came around in front of him and put her arms around him, pressing her cheek against his chest.

Her skin was cool to the touch and slightly clammy. Raider guessed that she was afraid. Of rejection now that she had offered herself to him? Possibly.

A disquieting thought came to him and he cleared his throat awkwardly. "Look, uh, Crystal . . ."

"Call me Chrys. Please? No one ever has before, but I like that ever so much more than Crystal." She giggled nervously. "I'm not breakable, you know." She raised her lips to his, but he pulled away from her and turned his head so that she kissed his cheek instead.

"Honey?" She sounded like she had begun to cry.

"I have to ask you something, Chrys."

"Uh huh."

"Is this . . . well . . . what I mean is, is your mother fixing to come in here and —"

"Honey, honest, I wouldn't try and trap you like that. I swear I wouldn't. I just . . . I asked Mama to give me some privacy. You know. Some time alone with you, without Charlie around all the time. If she had any idea that I . . . well, she'd be simply mortified. But it isn't anything like what you thought. I promise." She pressed nearer and kissed him again. This time he did not turn away.

The feel of her, naked and ripe in his arms, was having the effect she wanted. There would have been no way he could have hidden that from her. She was holding herself too tight against him for that.

She was a plain girl, true, but she looked just fine in the dark. He returned her kiss and discovered that she had left her spectacles behind somewhere.

He ran his hands down her body, and she shuddered with the pleasure of his touch.

Her breasts were melon-sized and soft. A few years from now they would be as droopy and flabby as her mothers. And those fell to the poor woman's waist. She likely had to take care that she didn't pinch her nipples whenever she put a belt on.

But now, at an age that Raider guessed to be somewhere in her late teens, Crystal's were ripe and ready.

He had gotten a glimpse of her in the flame of the match. Her nipples were large and pale. Raider toyed with them, rolling one and then the other between his thumb and finger. Crystal moaned and opened her mouth to his kiss.

"Could I . . . could I touch you?" Before he could answer she was fumbling awkwardly with his buttons. He helped and within moments was as naked as she.

She pressed against him again, finding him with her hands.

Her breath quickened and whistled slightly in a quick intake of air as she realized the size and the hardness of him. "I never . . ."

"You never what?"

She shook her head. "So big, that's all." She giggled and nuzzled her face into the hollow of his neck, still cupping and caressing him in both her hands. "It's almost like warm marble. It feels that smooth. I kind of thought it would be sort of, well, knobby. You know. Like a dog's."

"You've never seen one?"

"Haven't seen yours either," she reminded him. "But I'd like to. Would you mind?"

It was not the sort of request a gentleman could refuse. If Raider had been a gentleman. "I don't mind."

She giggled and kissed him again, then pulled away and left him. She was going back to the brass matchbox that hung beside the wall lamp. He heard the lid rattle, the same sound he had heard but had not been able to identify before, and she hurried back to him.

She knelt in front of him and struck the match.

"Not too close," he whispered.

She was peering too intently at him to speak, but she nodded as she leaned nearer, holding the match to one side and then the other as she examined his tool. She seemed positively fascinated by it. Her eyes were wide, and she was biting at her lower lip in concentration, as if she was trying to memorize every line and texture of it. She continued her inspection until the flame consumed the matchstick down to her fingers. Only then, with a low yelp of pain, did she shake it out.

She sighed. "That's the prettiest thing I ever saw, honey."

Raider chuckled and leaned down to take her by the arms and raise her to her feet so he could kiss her again. Her flesh was still cool to the touch, but it no longer felt clammy.

He explored inside her mouth with his tongue, and Crystal went limp in his arms.

Raider remembered seeing a leather-covered couch at the side of the room. Still holding her close, he maneuvered them to it and lowered Crystal until he was lying half on top of her.

He kneaded one huge breast with strong fingers, then shifted his hand lower. Her belly was soft and slightly rounded. She giggled when he probed inside her navel with a fingernail.

"That tickles."

"And this?" He moved the questing hand lower still.

Crystal moaned and opened herself to his touch. "No," she whispered, "that doesn't tickle.

"Should I stop?"

"No!" She grabbed the hand and pressed it against her vee. She was moist there and very warm.

Raider rubbed at her for a moment, then dipped a finger inside. She raised her hips to meet him. Getting even one finger inside was difficult. She was exceptionally tight, possibly—even probably—a virgin, yet there was no mistaking her eagerness or her desire.

Her breathing was heavier now, and she continued to clutch and pull at him with both hands.

She shifted position to give him easier access and began to laugh.

"Is something funny?"

"Kind of. But not you," she added quickly. "It's the way it feels when I move. The leather sticks to my skin and feels kind of strange. You know?"

"Mmmm." He sucked one firm nipple into his mouth and slid a second finger inside her. Crystal gasped and wriggled to capture more of him inside her straining body.

He raised his head from the twin pillows of her chest and grinned, even though he knew she couldn't see. "The good part is still to come, you know."

"If it feels any better than this, I'll just *die*. I know I will."

He chuckled and moved over her, between her parted thighs. Not for a moment did her constant touching and fondling slacken.

"Guide me inside now." He lowered himself gently to her.

Crystal lovingly petted the bulbous red head of his cock, then inserted it where it belonged. As Raider pressed forward into her she continued to stroke his shaft until there was nothing left for her to touch.

She groaned deep in her throat and wrapped her arms tight around him. "It is better. I wouldn't have believed it, but it really is." She sounded on the verge of tears.

She raised her hips to him. He could feel the hard ridge

of her pelvic bone. She was so tight it was as if she was still holding him, gripping with all her strength. He could feel hot moisture dripping onto his balls and suspected that at least some of it might be her blood from a man's first entry into that delightful place.

"Oh, Raider. Honey."

He began to stroke slowly in and out, shallow at first, giving her time to stretch and become comfortable. Then quicker and deeper, building slowly.

Crystal responded with eagerness if not with skill. As his strokes became stronger her breath became ragged, until she was gasping and clutching him fiercely.

Raider felt the rising tide of his climax and slowed a little, giving her time to catch up.

She did, quickly. He could feel it in the strong, spasmodic contractions and in the pattern of her breathing.

When she began to buck and shudder he let himself go, spilling over the final edge of control to pour his fluids into her in a long, almost continuous flow of hot release.

The intensity of it was so strong that it took him a few moments to realize that Crystal was sobbing beneath him.

He felt a pang of quick remorse. "Did I hurt you? Are you all right?"

"I'm fi . . . fi . . . fine," she gasped. "It was just so wonderful. I never imagined . . . I mean I . . ."

Raider chuckled, relieved. He bent and kissed her long and deep.

"Next time could be even better," he said. "Or maybe not. But the fun is in the findin' out."

Crystal sighed and pressed her cheek against his. "I'm willing to find out if you are," she whispered.

CHAPTER FOURTEEN

Maxwell Timmons was a small man, not at all what Raider had more or less expected—small and dapper and dressed like he was going for a promenade in the park instead of working cattle. He had closely cropped hair of a steel gray color and a neatly trimmed mustache. He wore a coat and tie and somewhat wilted collar even in the midst of the dust of moving a herd of perhaps fifty bovines.

The cattle were all bulls, Raider saw. And all the long-legged, slab-sided, tough and wiry old range breed. Nothing fancy about them.

Which was apparently the reason they were being brought in to the pens.

Timmons let his riders take over as they reached the corrals. He pulled his exceptionally tall and handsome saddle horse off to the side and watched with satisfaction as his crew worked the small herd of bulls into a stout and obviously new corral addition.

The man acknowledged his wife and daughter running out into the yard to greet him, but his attention was on the bulls and the men who were working them.

"There," he said with contentment as the last of the animals was shoved inside the enclosure and the gate was latched shut behind them. "That's the last of them."

He bent from his saddle to accept a welcome-home kiss on the cheek from his daughter and another, even briefer peck from his wife. Then he turned his attention to Raider.

"I presume you are the buyer, sir, from Slidel Packing Company?"

"Nope," Raider said. He introduced himself.

He was watching Timmons for a reaction at the mention of the Pinkerton Agency, but there was none. Or if there was it was so well contained that Raider could not see it.

"I was expecting a buyer for these bologna bulls."

"Come again?" Raider asked.

"You know. Bologna bulls. The only thing these old sons of bitches are good for is grinding up for bologna. Too tough for anything else, but they'll bring a fair price for that."

"You're stripping your herd of bulls?" Raider asked. It seemed a curious move when the man had just paid for the purchase of nine thousand head, mostly breeding stock.

"Not at all," Timmons said. "Upgrading. I have two carloads of Hereford"—he pronounced it in the British fashion, with three syllables in the word rather than the Americanized two—"bulls due in next week. I have to get rid of these, though, or they'll fight, and I fear my fine new Herefords would not fare so well against these beasts. Why do you ask?"

Raider shrugged. "Just curious."

Timmons grunted and stepped down from his saddle. For a man no taller than he was, and a horse that probably went seventeen hands or better, it was a long step down. As he dropped his reins in the dirt, a flushed, sweaty cowboy came rushing over to take them and lead the horse away toward another set of corrals. Raider found that interesting too. It was damned rare that a cowhand would consent to do menial work like fetching for another human being. And to have it done at a run was practically unthinkable.

Raider glanced toward Charlie Krepp, who was drifting toward them from the bunkhouse. As Raider had expected, even the kid was giving the Timmons rider a contemptuous look as the man trotted past with Timmons's horse in tow.

Timmons saw Charlie too. He dismissed him at first,

turning toward Raider with his lips parted and a question in his eyes. Then he turned back to look at Charlie again.

"I've seen you before, haven't I, young fellow?"

"Uh huh," Charlie grudgingly admitted.

Timmons's face clouded. "Now I remember. One of that Texan's riders." The man turned to spear Crystal with a sharp look and jerked his head toward the house. "Inside, young lady. Go with her, Mother."

Crystal started to protest, but her mother took her by the elbow and steered her toward the house.

There had been a certain amount of tension between Crystal and Charlie when they first got there, Raider recalled, but it hadn't seemed like anything of any importance. Apparently Timmons did not share that opinion. The man looked back at Charlie and scowled. "Now. You. Get the hell off my land. I told you before not to come back here. Leave now, sir, or by God I shall have you thrashed."

Raider noted that Timmons did not offer to do any of the thrashing himself. His threat was to have it done.

Charlie raised his chin defiantly. His jaw was set, and his lips were compressed. "I'm here with my friend Raider. I'm helpin' him and the Pinkertons to find Mr. Boatwright, so you by God *can't* order me off."

Timmons's threatening looks swung toward Raider. "Both of you leave. Right now. Off. Off my place. *Now.*"

"But Mr. Timmons . . ." Raider started.

The dapper little man got red in the face. His neck swelled, and if he had had hackles they damn sure would have been high.

"Get off. Right now. And take this scum with you."

"Look, Timmons, I don't know what this is all about, but I'm trying to—"

"I do not give a silver-plated shit *what* you are trying to do, sir. Get off my land, and take this miserable little bastard with you."

The bulls were all contained inside the nearby pen now, and the Timmons riders had been unsaddling, filling pipes, and rolling cigarettes nearby. At the sound of their employer's tone of voice they were beginning to tie their mounts to the corral rails and drift closer, spreading into a wide semicircle with Timmons, Charlie Krepp, and Raider focused in the center. Timmons appeared to be unarmed, but his riders were not. They looked like a hard crew. And there were more than a dozen of them.

"Get out," Timmons hissed again.

"It's about the disappearance of John Boatwright," Raider tried to inject.

But Timmons was not listening. "I don't give a crap about John Boatwright, and I know nothing about him, sir. Our business was concluded, and I have no further knowledge or interest in the man or in any of his people." He shifted his narrow-eyed look toward Charlie and added, "*especially* about any of his people. Now leave."

Timmons nodded toward a lanky man wearing sleeve garters, a soiled vest, and a dusty derby hat. The tall man might have looked ludicrous in that outfit, but the worn grips of his revolver and the confident air with which he wore the gun said that he had weathered enough storms about that in the past that the subject was not likely to be raised again.

"Give them five minutes to gather their things, Ralph," Timmons ordered. "If they're still here after that time, do whatever you must to evict them. And of course send for the sheriff. I shall be happy to press charges against them for trespass."

Ralph nodded and spat. "Sure thing, Mr. Timmons," he drawled. He was speaking to Timmons, but he was looking square into Raider's eyes.

Raider turned to square off facing Ralph, but the man slowly lifted his hands away from his belt and busied himself with rolling a smoke. "Five minutes," he said.

Raider was tempted. He could take this cocky SOB. He was sure of that. He could take him and probably half his friends as well.

But there would always be that other half of the crew still to go. They didn't look like a particularly friendly bunch at the moment.

Besides, damn it, he had no authority here. Unlike a

sworn peace officer, he had no legal right to search or question. Maxwell Timmons was on his own private property, and whatever suspicions Raider might have about the man meant nothing until or unless a court of law or a sworn officer said they had meaning.

At the moment Timmons had every legal right to throw Raider, Charlie Krepp, and the United States Cavalry off his property if he wanted to. And he obviously wanted to.

Raider sighed. This was a fight he could not win. If it came to gunplay and he won that part of the game, Timmons would still beat him. A word to the county sheriff would see to that.

Raider and young Krepp had no choice about it but to leave, exactly when and as Maxwell Timmons demanded.

Shit, Raider grumbled silently. He made sure his expression did not change when he thought it. He was *not* going to give Slick-gun Ralph that kind of satisfaction. But he was beaten and he knew it.

For the moment.

"Come on, Charlie," he muttered. "Get your gear together."

"But, Rade . . ."

"Damn it, Charlie, I said get your gear together. We only got four minutes left to get off this, uh, *gentleman's* fucking property."

Raider saw the smirk that spread across the thin face of the man called Ralph. It was all Raider could do to keep from turning and kicking the son of a bitch in the nuts. Just to take that expression off him.

But he managed it somehow. He did not like it. Not worth a damn. But right now he had no choice about it.

Instead he gave Charlie Krepp a shove between the shoulder blades to get him moving toward the bunkhouse.

Shit, Raider said to himself again.

CHAPTER FIFTEEN

Doc left the saloon and stepped down off the board sidewalk into the dust of the narrow street. He was far from being satisfied with the way his evening was going, although he truly had expected no less. The liquor in the place had been acceptable, but the conversation was not. As he had more than half expected after striking out back in Ogallala, no one in Beam's Crossing remembered seeing anything of John Boatwright or any member of his crew.

After Doc checked the two of them into the only hotel in the town, he had spent the remainder of the afternoon poking around at the livery stable, the backyard horse sheds, and the public hitch racks in the community, but there was no sign of any of the horses young Krepp had described to him. He was having the same poor luck now when he asked townspeople about the missing men.

It was all unproductive so far, but that was simply part of the job. A hundred useless inquiries might be required before one solid lead turned up in any investigation, and this search for John Boatwright was no exception to that rule. He turned left, heading for the last of the several saloons in town. He had little hope of success there either, but the attempt would have to be made. Weatherbee permitted himself no less than his best efforts on any job.

He sighed as he walked, acknowledging that he would give Angela Boatwright his best on this job too. But that was a matter of his own pride and *not* from any sense of obligation to that strange woman. She hadn't spoken to him since the scene in her hotel room back in Ogallala and was quite obviously still harboring a grudge about his refusal to succumb to her charms.

Tough, he thought. That was a complication he didn't need.

He neared the last block of commercial buildings on the short street that made up the business district of the small river town and angled toward the boardwalk that ran along the front of them. Signs hung on the storefronts proclaiming the services of a harness maker, a land agent, and the saloon. Of the three, only the saloon was open for business at this hour. The other windows were dark, their glass reflecting only the last dying light of the evening sky.

"That's him." The voice was a rasping, whiskey whisper that came from Doc's left, from the narrow, weedy vacant lot that separated the block of buildings from the next group closer to the town center. The sound carried clearly on the still air and almost certainly was not intended to reach Doc's ears.

He stopped and waited. A moment later two men stepped out of the shadows. They were hulking, nondescript men dressed in rough clothing. One of them carried a bottle, which he set carefully aside, placing it on the ground beside the east wall of a closed and empty storefront. Beam's Crossing was not booming. Several business locations in that next-to-last block were empty, with fading signs advertising businesses that had gone under.

Doc noticed that, almost ignoring the two men who faced him. The pair did not seem worthy of much attention anyway. They had been drinking and were well on toward being drunk. They were both smirking, sharing some private joke or intention.

Intention, Doc decided as he watched the way they moved toward him.

These imbeciles intended to give him a thrashing.

They were not armed—not with revolvers, at any rate, he saw. Apparently they felt that bulk and foul odor should be enough to overwhelm any opponent. Doc's nose wrinkled as they came nearer to him. They might be right at that. At least about their combined stench overcoming opposition. They were a rank pair, and that was a fact.

"I take it you, uh, gentlemen have been looking for me," Doc said mildly.

The two seemed to find that highly amusing. They looked at each other and grinned, and one of them jabbed the other with the point of his elbow.

"The little feller thinks we been lookin' for him," one of them said to his companion. He turned to fix Doc with a stare that probably was intended to be intimidatingly scary. "Now why would we do a thing like that?"

"Actually," Doc said, "I have no idea. Why would you?"

The man, slightly the larger of the pair, almost choked on his own laughter.

"We ain't been lookin' for you," the other one said, "but I expect we found you. So what ought we t' do about that now that we got you?"

Both of them cracked up with laughter over the possibilities now that Doc had been found.

"Got any ideas about that, little feller?"

That was the second time one of them had referred to Weatherbee as little. He was beginning to find that annoying. He was not a very large man, true, but neither was he small.

"He sho' looks fancy, don' he, Dan?" the bigger of them asked.

"Sure does."

"Most too fancy for around here."

"We could muss him up some."

"Fit in better if we did."

"It'd practic'ly be doin' him a favor."

"You'd like us to do you a favor, wouldn't you, little feller?" They were both grinning at him, Dan and the other one, whatever his name was.

Doc smiled back at them blandly. They started toward him, but he noticed a lady approaching on the street, apparently walking from one of the houses that rimmed the town and coming toward the center of the business district. He didn't want a lady to have to witness a public brawl.

"Join me, gentlemen?" Doc invited politely. He slipped between them and stepped into the shadows of the vacant lot, off the public street and more or less out of public view there.

Dan and his partner chuckled and followed behind.

Doc was walking ahead of the pair, his back to them, but he was not as unwary as they might have believed. He listened closely, expecting and soon hearing an abrupt change in the rhythm of their footfalls as one of them lunged toward his back as he passed into the shadows.

Doc sidestepped to his left and swung his right fist in a backhanded arch that caught the unsuspecting Dan high on the bridge of his nose. Dan sprawled face down in the dirt and litter of the vacant lot, blood already streaming from his broken nose. His partner seemed to get quite a kick out it and began laughing.

"The little feller too much for you, Danny?" he yelped.

Dan staggered to his feet with both hands clamped over his face in a futile attempt to stop the flow of blood. His partner was still laughing. Doc stood calmly waiting for them, his back prudently to the wall of the empty building.

"Let me show you how you're s'posed to do this, Danny," the uninjured ruffian said. He turned to Doc with a leer of eager anticipation on his face. He needed a shave and a haircut, Doc noted.

The man balled his hands into fists and came forward.

Doc raised his own fists in the approved manner, and the man began to laugh again.

"D'you see that, Danny? The little feller figgers to fight me, b'God. Marquis o' Queensbury rules an' everything." Still laughing, he moved closer. Doc waited and let him come.

The man reared back and threw a powerful straight right hand directly toward the point of Doc's jaw. If the blow had landed it would have ended the contest on the spot.

But that was only if it landed.

Doc's left forearm flicked up and to the side, almost casually brushing the other man's wrist to the side and diverting his punch harmlessly away. Doc didn't even give the man the satisfaction of ducking away from the blow.

"I'll be go to hell," the fellow said.

He looked slightly puzzled but still more amused than anything else. He took his time about setting his feet, then threw a left and quickly behind it another crushing right hand.

Again Doc's forearms darted up to deflect the blows and send them wide. Still he waited. Doc had yet to throw a punch of his own.

Behind the man, Danny was getting some sense back and was moving in to join his friend.

The big man tried an uppercut next. Doc swayed to his right, and the man's fisted hand whistled harmlessly past his jaw.

This time, though, Doc stepped forward. The hard flat of his left fist jabbed out and out and out again, bouncing painfully off the point of the big man's nose and bringing blood to his nostrils and tears to his eyes. The jabs would sting like hell. Worse, they were humiliating. This dapper, fancy-dressed fellow was not *cooperating*.

With a howl of anger, the big man lowered his head and made a bull-like lunge forward, both arms extended wide apart to capture and crush Weatherbee.

Doc feinted left with his upper body, then quickly darted to his right. The big man rushed past him and crashed headfirst into the wooden slabs of the wall behind Doc.

Good construction, Doc thought. The sound of the impact thudded like a bass drum, but the planks held. The big man went down like a poleaxed steer, dropping face first to the ground with a split in his scalp that poured blood.

Doc didn't have time to admire the results of the charge. Danny bellowed and jumped forward with his fists flailing.

Doc picked off one swing after another, calm and methodical about it. One blow nearly got through. It ripped across Doc's right ear in a glancing rush. It stung enough to piss Doc off.

Doc grunted and stepped forward, his feet shuffling quickly so that his balance was never disrupted. He jabbed with his left—one, two, four quick, sharp punches—then followed with a right to the jaw.

The right caught Danny coming in. It landed flush and staggered him. His eyes became glassy, and he had a boyishly innocent expression as the cares of the world were softened and began to recede.

Doc moved forward and to his right, waited until Dan was perfectly positioned, and then set him down in the weeds with a hard right to the temple. Dan hit the ground crosslegged, wobbled there for a moment, and went over on his back with his arms thrown wide and that innocent expression still on his face. He began to snore.

"Are we done now?" Doc asked the other man, who by now was on his knees with a filthy—and now blood-crusted—bandanna pressed over the split in his scalp.

The man did not look much inclined to continue the fight; but Doc was not going to make any silly assumptions along those lines.

The man blinked owlishly and peered first at his partner and then at Doc. "You sonuvabitch, you ain't even lost your hat."

"I'd rather you didn't call me that again," Doc said mildly. "It tends to make me angry."

The man glared at him but said nothing. He made it to his feet on the second attempt and wobbled to his partner's side.

"I'd like to have a talk with you about why we had this little dance," Doc said.

"Go to hell." The man slapped his partner several times and eventually succeeded in bringing him more or less around. The man got Dan's arm over his shoulders, and between them, one braced against the other, they got to their knees and finally upright.

The two of them staggered off into the dusk. Doc watched them go, then shrugged and turned toward the one saloon he had not yet visited. He still had work to do here, after all.

But he was curious about why a pair of such obvious toughs had been lying in wait for him. It made no sense that their assault would be connected with the disappearance of John Boatwright and his quarter million dollars. Anyone involved in the theft of that much money and the number of murders it would require to carry it off would surely not hesitate about one more murder. And an ambush is nearly always more effective than this kind of asinine performance.

Even so, Doc reminded himself, he really should start carrying his .38 from here on in. Just in case he was stepping on toes that he was not aware of.

He entered the last saloon, and the thought of a mellow brandy presented itself attractively as the sights and smells surrounded him.

CHAPTER SIXTEEN

They entered the tree line, drawn across the foot of the low hill with an engineer's precision at the sharp separation between grass flat and treed slope, and pulled to a halt some twenty yards inside the cover of the evergreens.

"Why are we stopping?" Charlie Krepp asked.

"I want to take a look down our back trail," Raider said. He turned his horse and edged it slowly toward the open flat again, just far enough that he could see the rolling, grassy country they had just come across, without being seen by anyone who might be back there.

"Are we being followed?" Charlie asked. He sounded more excited by the possibility than worried about it.

Raider shrugged. "Don't know, exactly. I just have a feeling. But if anybody is trailing us, they're damned good."

"Yeah?" Charlie fumbled in the pouch at his belt—in spite of all the trimming and modifying he had done on the thing, it still didn't deserve to be called a holster—and eventually found the butt of his beat-up old revolver.

"Put that thing away, damn it," Raider said. "If anybody is back there, I just want to know about it. That's *all*. You understand me?"

"Anything you say, Rade," Charlie said. He stuffed the ancient Colt back into its pouch and stood in his stirrups, straining to see if anyone was coming along behind them.

"Not right out there where we was," Raider told him. "I already tol' you, if anyone is following us, he's damn good at it. So he wouldn't be coming direct the way we already rode. He'd be flanking our trail. Following, but way the hell off to the side. Just so's a pup like you wouldn't be able to see him. You keep an eye on the top o' that rise over there," Raider said, pointing, "an' I'll watch over to that side. And don't be looking for a horse and rider, neither. If you see anything at all it'll likely be no more than a hat or the flick of a horse's ears. If anyone's back there, and I sure got the feeling there might be, he's too good to show himself."

"You can count on me, Rade."

Raider grunted. He had some doubts about that. The kid was just such a . . . *kid*. At least there was a cure for that. Time. If the damn fool lived that long.

Raider saw nothing, not in the area he had told Charlie he would be watching nor in the sector where young Krepp was supposed to be watching. Raider knew better than to totally trust the unpracticed eyes of a youngster like Charlie, so he was doing all the watching that counted himself. Still, he wanted the boy to feel useful, so he had given him a chore. The kid would have no way to know that it was only a make-work proposition.

Raider definitely had the feeling that someone from the Timmons place had followed and was making sure they were leaving the ranch, as Maxwell Timmons had ordered. It was nothing Raider could prove, but he felt it in his gut. That was more than enough reason to believe it.

And it certainly was what Raider himself would have done if things had been reversed and he were the one trying to hide a dark secret like counterfeiting and murder. *If* he was right about that.

After several minutes Raider kept his eyes along both sides of the back trail but spoke to his young companion.

"What is it that Timmons has against you, kid?"

"Nothing, Rade. Honest." Raider did not turn to see the wide-eyed, innocent expression Charlie would be giving him. He didn't have to. He knew it would be there.

"Bullshit," Raider said mildly.

"No. Really."

"Bullshit. The girl acted a little funny when we got there too, now that I think on it. So what happened?"

"Aw, that. Hell, Rade, that wasn't nothing to get excited about."

Raider grunted.

"All it was," Charlie said, "was that I, well, I kinda told her I'd taken a shine to her. And I guess I kind of, you know, kind of slipped—my hand, I mean—and I kind of, well, touched her. Just a little." He whistled and rolled his eyes although Raider did not see that. "Them titties, Rade. Have you ever seen anything like them tits?"

"In other words," Raider said, "you groped the damned girl, is that it?"

"No," Charlie protested. He sounded wounded by the mere thought of such an accusation. "I never. My hand, it just slipped, like I said, and kind of . . . *brushed* her chest. That's all. Hell, Rade, I know better'n to grab at her titties. 'Specially a girl with a daddy as rich as hers. I mean, shit, Rade, a fella could wallow in them tits like a hog in a mudhole, and if he married her, well, he'd be set for life. You know?"

Raider shook his head. The ignorant kid had actually groped her. Likely out of the clear blue, without even a word of sweet-talk or warning. Dumb.

Aside from being dumb, though, it put a crimp in the ideas Raider had been getting about Maxwell Timmons and the man's insistence that they leave his property immediately. Sure, it would be logical for Timmons to throw them off the place if he was a thief and a murderer and possibly a counterfeiter too. But it would be just as logical for Timmons to throw young Charlie Krepp off the place *and* any of his friends if the damn fool kid already was known to have taken a crack at Timmons's darling daughter.

Dumb damn kid, Raider told himself again.

"Are we goin' on down to Three Trees next?" Charlie asked, obviously wanting to change the subject.

"Three Trees? Where's that?"

"Next town down toward the Belle Fourche," Charlie said. "It's where Mr. John told the boys they could have their blowout on the way home."

"You never told us about that before."

"I'd forgot until we got up here, and I got to remembering some things. You know. About when I was here before with all the other boys. They was really looking forward to it, but of course I was going on down to Denver and wasn't paying all that much attention to what they was planning."

"We'll get around to that," Raider said. "Or Doc will check it out if he gets there before we do."

"What're we going to do, then?"

"First thing, we need to shake off our tail. I still feel like there's somebody following. We got to convince him— or them, but I'd guess at just one man because I can't imagine finding two fellows on the same outfit that'd be so damned good at not being seen—anyway, we got to shake him off, then slip back here and do some looking on the Timmons grass."

"Why's that, Rade?"

"I been thinking, Charlie, and if anybody was able to jump Boatwright and his crew and get them all, which would take some pretty fancy doing, but say somebody was able to manage it, why, they'd have a hell of a time disposing of all those bodies. They'd have to do something with them, though. So what I want to do before we cut away from here and get on down the line, I want us to take a look in every coulee and washout on the Timmons range. See if any of them have been broke down along the walls or like that."

"I don't understand," Krepp said.

"Think about it, boy. A grave big enough to hold all those bodies would take a fucking week to dig and half of another to fill up. That many people to bury, you'd want to use a natural hole of some kind. Like lay them at the bottom of a wash and knock the bank down over them. Something like that. So that's what we'll be looking for."

"Something like that will take a whole lot of riding and looking," Charlie said.

"If you have anything better to do," Raider told him, "have at it."

"No, sir."

"All right, then."

They continued their watch along the back trail for a full hour and then for a little while longer just in case.

Finally Raider relaxed his attention and turned to look at Charlie Krepp.

"We head back onto Timmons's grass?" Charlie asked.

"Nope," Raider said. "Now we point south. Toward—what was it you said that town is named?"

"Three Trees?"

Raider nodded. "That's the place."

"But I thought you said we wasn't going there?"

Raider smiled at him. "I did. And we aren't. But I also said we have to lose whoever's following us. And I want him to believe we're going to Three Trees."

"But there isn't anybody—"

"Kid, we didn't *see* anybody. That don't tell me that there ain't anybody. Only that he's damned good at what he's doing. So what we got to do is be even better at getting rid of him than he is at staying with us."

Charlie looked at Raider with open admiration. "You sure know what you're doing, Rade. I swear, I'm just so damn proud that you and me are friends. So proud o' that that I could just bust, I swear it."

"You'll learn," Raider said. Which might or might not be a lie but which couldn't hurt.

He turned his horse away, heading south through the stand of thick timber in the direction this Three Trees was supposed to be in. "Come on, Charlie. And stay with me, hear? I don't want to lose you while I'm losing Timmons's rider back there."

"You bet," Charlie said eagerly. He bumped his horse forward until his right stirrup was knocking against Raider's left with every other step.

Raider groaned silently to himself. He hadn't meant for the damn kid to stay *that* close.

CHAPTER SEVENTEEN

Raider tossed his empty can into the hole Charlie had dug and wiped his hands on the seat of his trousers. He was getting purely tired of canned shit. But that had never been enough to discourage him before, and it wasn't likely to send him packing now.

They hadn't yet seen quite all of the Timmons range, but they had damn sure been working at it. Five days now, counting the one they had spent going up to Wolf Point for the canned goods and bread that was now stale and hard almost to the point of being inedible. They hadn't built a fire or fired a gun since they returned to the Timmons grass— either was much too likely to be noticed by the working hands who drifted across the grass on obscure missions for their boss—and the cold food and empty blankets were tiresome.

Still, there was a job to be done.

Raider had more than half expected Charlie Krepp to become so disillusioned that he begged off from this part of the hunt, but the damned kid seemed to be glorying in it. He acted like every boring minute was exciting. And at night he fondled that silly, antique pistol like it was his best girl.

"Can I cover the hole in now?" Charlie asked once the

last of the empty cans had been disposed of underground.

Raider nodded and started to speak, but Charlie cut him short.

"I know. I'll hide it with leaves an' shit just the way you showed me."

Raider nodded again and bent to pick up his canteen. The water was fresh—lack of water would never be a problem on the Timmons spread—and should have tasted good, but after drinking nothing else for so many days it was flat and uninteresting. By now Raider would gladly have wrestled a bear for a cup of campfire coffee. And he'd have been willing to do it with *both* arms tied behind his back.

"Where to this morning?" Charlie asked as he finished sifting a handful of dead pine needles over the spot where their garbage hole had been dug.

Raider shrugged. "North again. We didn't get a look into that side cut yesterday evening."

"Just down from where you saw that crippled cow?"

"Uh huh."

"All right." Charlie finished his chore, wiped his hands, and bounced to his feet. "I'll get the horses." The animals were kept on a short picket rope deep in the stunted trees. It gave them little feed at night and meant a long nooning each day so they could graze, but it made sure they wouldn't wander and attract the attention of some passing cowhand's mount. Raider was reasonably certain they had convinced Timmons's man that they had left the country heading south. He didn't want to confuse anyone with the truth at this point. Not until he had had a chance to check every likely burial site he could locate.

The kind of country they were looking for made keeping out of sight of the Timmons hands easier. The cowboys were interested in riding the ridges, up where they could see more country and keep an eye on things that needed doing. Raider and Krepp were riding the bottoms of the washes, looking for any places where rock or dirt falls had been pushed down to cover the remains of the men and animals from the Boatwright crew. So far it seemed to be working out.

Charlie led the horses back to where the cold camp had been, and they saddled in silence except for the creak of leather and the pop of cinch straps being yanked tight.

"Ready?" Raider asked.

Charlie swung onto his horse and nodded.

"Let's go, then."

Raider paused at the edge of the timber to study the skyline and make double damn sure there was no one in sight. Then he led them downslope at a quick trot, as fast as they could comfortably move without raising dust, and into the bottom of a deep wash. There was a thread of water running through the center of the wash. Raider stopped there to let the horses drink before they moved on, still keeping to the bottom of the high-walled cut. A Timmons rider could have been fifty yards away on the flat grass above them but would not have been able to see down into the bottom where Raider and Charlie moved.

They reached the fork Raider remembered from the evening before, a point where the spring melt roaring off two different hillsides met to form the deep main wash. They angled to the right into the secondary cut.

"This one ain't real likely," Raider observed after they had ridden no more than a few hundred yards. Already the sides of the wash were only shoulder high to a man on horseback, and the cut quickly became even more shallow ahead of them.

"Not enough of a bank to cover that many men and animals if they broke both sides down," Raider observed.

"I sure as hell hope we find 'em today."

"You do?" Raider turned and gave his young companion a questioning look.

The kid blushed. "I don't mean I wish 'em dead. Or nothing like that. I just meant . . . well, you know . . ."

"Yeah," Raider grunted. "I know." So maybe the kid wasn't as eager as he acted. Raider reined his horse back down toward the deep main branch of the wash, which would have been called an arroyo in other parts of the West. "Let's look for some new country."

"Come to think of it," Charlie said with a grin, "I hope

we don't find nothing we have to dig up today." He looked at his palms, where some blisters were just beginning to heal.

So far they had found only two places where fallen bank sides might have hidden something, but it had taken the two of them hours to dig out enough rock and soil at each of those places to show that there was nothing more sinister buried there than weeds and gravel. The cave-ins had occurred naturally or perhaps were caused by an incautious cow walking over the undercut tops of the banks. It had taken hard work to determine that, though.

Raider grunted and moved back down into the protection of the high side walls where they could not be seen so easily.

He heard something and pulled his horse to a halt.

"What . . .?"

Raider shook his head and motioned Krepp to be quiet. He was not sure what he had heard. It might have been the discharge of a small-caliber rifle or pistol. Nothing louder than a .22 though. And who in hell would be carrying a .22 out here?

He heard it again. And then quickly again. He still wasn't sure what it was.

"What the fuck would that be?"

"Sounds like one of them little gallery rifles," Charlie said.

"That doesn't make sense."

"You reckon we should ride the other way?"

Raider shook his head. "I want to see what it is." The sound had come from off to the right, somewhere up the main branch of the wash. Raider turned his horse that way, and Charlie followed. Raider noticed that he rode with one hand on his reins and the other resting on the butt of his old pistol.

They heard the sharp thin report again and yet again. It came from down inside the wash, around a bend or two in front of them. Raider pulled his horse to a stop and threw his reins to Charlie.

"Wait here. If I come fogging it afoot down this bottom,

boy, don't you for damn sure turn loose of my horse until I have him, you hear?"

"Yes, sir." Charlie pulled his revolver.

"An' put that damn thing back where it belongs. Damn, boy, but you make me nervous with that thing."

Charlie grinned at him but stuffed the pistol back into its pouch.

As a precaution Raider pulled his Winchester from the scabbard on his saddle and carried it with him.

There was that sound again. Closer now. It still sounded like a little rimfire gallery rifle. Perhaps some young'un was having target practice shooting at dirt clods. If so, Raider would get a look and then slide quietly away without the kid ever being the wiser. But he wanted to know whatever it was that was happening.

Raider eased along the edge of the wash bottom where the soil was mostly sand and quiet to walk in. He reached the shoulder of the bend in the wash, removed his hat, and peeped around to see into the next straight stretch of bottom.

He began to boil almost immediately.

That son of a bitch!

There were six people he could see down in the bottom there; a single ground-reined horse stood patiently on the grass above.

Five raggedy-assed Indians.

And the Timmons rider called Ralph.

The Indians were cowered together in a forlorn little clump of humanity, pushed up against the side of the wall—one man, a scrawny fellow with a withered arm and clothes that were rags, and a pair of equally miserable-looking women. The three adults were huddled over two thoroughly frightened children.

Ralph stood ten feet or so away from the group of scared, bleeding Indians.

The sound Raider had heard was the popping of a slender whip that Ralph carried.

The son of a bitch was using it too, even though the Indians were defenseless and making no attempt to resist.

Ralph looked like he was enjoying himself. He flicked the tip of the whip out along the ground behind him and said something that was too low for Raider to hear, then he swung it forward in a slow, lazy roll.

The tip of the lash floated forward as the whip doubled on itself and moved out in front almost to full extension. Then Ralph jerked up and back with his wrist, and the rawhide popper snapped.

A cut appeared in the thin cloth that covered the Indian man's right shoulder, and within moments the gap was filled with an ooze of bright blood. The Indian made no sound and did not move except to try and wrap himself more completely around the shoulders of the two women. He was trying to protect them from the whip just as they were trying to protect the children. He didn't make a sound, but Raider thought he could hear Ralph chuckle.

Cocksucker, Raider thought. He probably enjoyed pulling the wings off flies too. With only one arm the poor damned Indian couldn't do much to defend his family, and Ralph knew it. Bastard.

Raider looked at the son of a bitch, and for an instant two distinctly separate inclinations warred within him. If he went out and showed himself to Timmons's man, all the secrecy of their being here would be blown to shit.

But if he stood here and let that prick use a whip to cut up five defenseless people . . .

Fuck it!

Raider stepped out into the bottom of the wash.

Ralph was concentrating so hard on his fun with the Indians that he didn't hear Raider behind him.

From this new angle Raider could see what had likely started the problem. A dead, half-butchered fat cow was lying on the floor of the wash. Raider knew without looking that one of the cow's legs was broken and probably another. He and Charlie had seen the animal the evening before.

Ralph chuckled again and tossed the whip out behind him along the ground, ready for another snap.

Raider's heel pinned the rawhide popper to the ground,

holding it there, and Ralph moved his arm to bring the lash sweeping forward.

The unexpected resistence snatched the handle of the whip from his hand as the tip remained pinned under Raider's boot heel.

"What the . . .?"

Ralph whirled. His hand was already moving toward the butt of his holstered revolver. He stopped, his eyes wide, when he saw the gaping muzzle of Raider's Remington pointed dead on his belt buckle.

"You aren't supposed to be here," he blurted.

"But I am."

"But . . ."

"I don't expect you to explain yourself here," Raider said, "so let me tell you what happened."

"But . . ."

"Shut up," Raider snapped. He motioned toward the still cowering Indians. "You came along and found these folks butchering that cow over there. They likely tried to tell you that the critter was already dead or dying when they found it, but you said they was lying. You said they was stealing a fat cow and you were gonna teach them a lesson. Well, listen to me, asshole. I saw that cow yesterday. It had fell over the bank and was already broke-legged and crippled. It was dead or dying when they found it, and God knows anybody can look at them and see they need the meat. So they wasn't doing anything wrong when they set in to butcher it. They were hungry, they got no guns to hunt with, and they were just gonna eat meat that would have laid there to rot if they hadn't come along. But you, you son of a bitch, you were gonna teach them a lesson." Raider smiled at him, but there was damn sure neither mirth nor humor in the expression. It was cold and deadly.

"You called me a son of a bitch," Ralph protested.

"That's right, I certainly did," Raider agreed.

"If you didn't have the drop on me . . ."

Raider let the hammer of the Remington down and dropped the revolver into his holster. "Uh huh?"

Ralph swallowed, hard, and glanced over his shoulder. But there was no crew of armed riders to back him this time. He was alone. And the big fish in the small pond suddenly found himself swimming in deeper waters than he wanted to.

"You want me to draw on you, don't you?"

"Let's just say that I wouldn't mind it if you did."

Ralph swallowed again, checked over his shoulder again. The rest of the crew was nowhere around. The only witnesses were the five wide-eyed Indians who still had not moved out of their protective huddle against the bank.

"There's a better way," Ralph said. He sounded hoarse, and the words came out in a croak.

Ralph used his left hand to carefully unbuckle his gunbelt and toss it aside. He looked like he felt considerably better once he was unarmed.

"You don't have any better chance that way, Ralph, but I don't give a shit. So what'll it be, Ralph? A knife maybe?"

The Timmons rider pointed toward his discarded gunbelt. A sheathed knife hung from it. "Bare hands," he said.

"All right." Raider unfastened his own belt and set it carefully aside. Any asshole who threw a loaded gun around was asking for trouble.

Raider straightened and squared off facing Ralph. "Anytime you're ready." He grinned.

But Ralph was grinning too.

Instead of charging toward Raider he stooped and snatched up the handle of the whip. The long lash snaked out behind him ready for its stinging snap.

Raider crossed his wrists in front of his eyes to protect them and balanced on the balls of his feet.

One cut. There was no way he could prevent the son of a bitch from getting one cut at him. But there might not be another. Not if Raider could get inside the lash faster than Ralph could back away from him.

Raider braced himself for the hot sting of the vicious lash and stepped forward.

Ralph's arm snapped forward.

Raider stopped. And began to laugh.

For the second time that morning, Ralph was standing with his hand empty, his whip on the ground and a stupid expression on his lean face.

The Indian that Ralph had been so happily whipping just minutes before had reached out and grabbed the tip of Ralph's blacksnake when the man pulled it back in that direction for the cut at Raider.

Now the Indian quickly hauled the whip in, hand over hand, until he had it bunched against his chest. The Indian had no expression on his face, but there was a certain glint in his eye as he took the whip out of the play.

Raider grinned, first at the Indian, then at Ralph. Then he began to stalk lightly forward with his fists ready.

"My oh my, Ralph," he whispered. "You done made you a mistake."

CHAPTER EIGHTEEN

The bartender scrubbed absently at the glass mug in his hands, polishing it over and over while he thought. After a moment he shook his head. "No, I don't recall seeing anybody like that in town. And like I already told you, I know for sure those names don't ring no bells with me. I don't believe they've been here."

Doc thanked the man for his help, paid for the beer he had barely tasted, and left. He was disappointed but not surprised. The story was the same here as he had heard already in Rapid City and in every other town and ranch they had passed to the south.

No one had seen John Boatwright. No one had seen any of Boatwright's men. No one had heard anything about that crew or anything like them.

With a sigh Doc acknowledged that he believed the people he had talked with. A quarter of a million dollars will buy a great deal of silence. But no thief could buy an entire populace. And *no* one admitted to having seen the Boatwright crew. Not anywhere they had yet been.

Obviously, the men had never gotten this far south on their trip home.

He headed back toward the hotel and supper, thinking about the case more than about where he was going. He almost ran into Angela Boatwright, who was just emerging from a store with her arms full of paper-wrapped bundles.

Doc's apology died stillborn in his throat. He and Mrs. Boatwright were still speaking only from the strictest necessity, although on those occasions when they were forced to spend a night on the road the damned woman was blatantly immodest. She seemed to delight in exposing herself whenever there was the slightest chance he could see.

She was not content with showing a flash of ankle, either. She would display her limbs thigh high. Or one breast would accidentally-on-purpose fall out of her wrapper. She didn't even bother to look for a bush when they were alone, just hiked her skirts to her waist and let it splash.

But she would not speak a civil word to him, and at this point he would give none to her. Damn her.

And the worst part of it all was that she was such a damned good-looking woman.

She was a beauty. But a bitch.

It would be fair to say that she was well along toward frazzling Weatherbee's good humor.

But at least there had been no repeats of that ambush by the unsavory types back in whatever the hell that town had been.

When Doc had showed up back at the hotel that evening Angela had given him a guarded look that Doc thought might have been one of surprise. He more than half suspected that she had arranged the waylaying herself, for her own vengeful reasons, and that it had nothing to do with his search for John Boatwright.

He couldn't prove that, of course, but he suspected it.

This time, outside the shop, the woman did choose to speak to him before he could get away.

"There you are. Good. I have better things to do than to look for you."

"Look for me? What for?" He knew better than to think she wanted to eat with him. They hadn't taken a meal together, except when forced to by being on the road far from anyplace where they could stop, since they'd left Ogallala.

"Pay the lady inside," she ordered in that haughty, ice princess tone of hers.

"Why should I pay for your things?" he snapped back at her.

She looked down her nose at him. "I brought limited traveling funds, if you must know. Although I certainly do *not* have to explain myself to you. Now go inside and do as I say. Mr. Pinkerton shall be receiving a full report of this affair, I assure you." She sniffed once and marched away toward the hotel, still loaded down with her purchases.

Doc watched her go in disgust. He was quite sure there would be a report made and was equally sure it would not be a flattering one.

Bad joss to her, damn her eyes.

He sighed again and hunched his shoulders. But there was no help for it. Pinkerton himself had said they were to go to any extreme in this case. That probably included following around after John Boatwright's bitch and paying her bills from now on. In addition to everything else.

Damn her.

She had shopped in every burg and crossroads they had passed since leaving Ogallala, and still she was shopping. He couldn't imagine what she could find to buy in all these badger holes and knew for a fact that if she assembled much more in the way of baggage they would have to either get a larger wagon for their travels or begin shipping trunks down to Texas just to get rid of the overflow. But still she shopped.

And now he was having to pay for it.

Grumbling and fussing under his breath, Doc shouldered his way inside the store.

Two customers and a salesgirl stopped talking in mid-sentence to gape at him.

He looked around and realized for the first time that the shop was one dealing in ladies' apparel. Possibly he was the first male who had walked through that door since the place had opened for business.

The women in the place turned their heads quickly. One

of the customers was blushing. She quickly dropped a pink lacy corset that she had been admiring, and both customers turned toward the doorway and brushed hurriedly past Doc on their way out. He was not at all embarrassed about being here, but apparently that degree of self-assurance did not extend to the customers.

The salesgirl blushed in sympathy with the departed customer, bobbed her head in Doc's direction, and fled toward the back room of the place.

A moment later a somewhat older woman appeared. Doc guessed that she would be the proprietor of the establishment.

"May I help you, sir?" she asked as if it were the most normal thing possible to find a man in her shop.

"Yes, I understand I have a bill to pay here."

"A . . . oh." The woman smiled. "You must mean for the lady from New Orleans."

Doc raised an eyebrow. "The, uh, lady I mean is from Texas, ma'am. A Mrs. Boatwright."

"But she said . . . never mind. I shall be glad to help you, Mr. Boatwright."

"My name is *not* Boatwright," Doc quickly corrected, "and I am only here as a courtesy." He introduced himself.

The shop owner smiled. He had not realized until then how stiffly and formally she was holding herself.

The woman was quite attractive when she smiled.

Doc guessed her to be somewhere in her thirties, with a few strands of graying hair showing in the bun that had been pulled tight and proper at the back of her head. Except for that her hair was a soft brown, almost blonde.

She was slender and quite tall, almost as tall as Doc. Her features were delicate, patrician. She had a cool, quiet beauty that was not commanding—almost hidden, in fact—but which seemed to grow with every new look he gave her.

Her clothing would have been fashionable in Boston, much less here in Spearfish. Her bustle and the loose bodice of her dress made it impossible for him to guess at the figure that lay beneath the cloth.

Yet after all the frustrations Angela Boatwright had imposed on him, Doc was finding himself doing a great deal of guessing about this elegantly attractive woman. He openly took a look at her left hand. Her fingers, long and slim, were bare of rings.

When he looked from the ring hand back to her eyes there was a slight crinkling of amusement there, and he thought he saw the ghost of a smile tugging at the corners of her lips.

"Shall we attend to business, Mr. Weatherbee?"

"Of course, Mrs., uh . . . ?"

"It is miss, sir. Miss Faith Hope." She laughed lightly. "Awful but true."

Doc leaned on the counter and looked into her eyes. They were a pale brown, he realized. In the softened light that came through the street-side window they looked almost yellow. "I hesitate to ask, but your middle name couldn't be Charity, could it?"

Miss Hope laughed again. "Can you keep a secret, Mr. Weatherbee?"

"Absolutely."

"Then I shall trust you with the truth. It is indeed Faith Charity Hope."

Doc swept his hat off and laughed with her. "Then surely, Miss Hope, I have never met a more virtuous damsel. Nor," he added, "a lovelier one."

Miss Hope did not merely laugh this time. She threw her head back and positively roared.

The sound brought the salesgirl to the back doorway. She poked her head through the curtained doorframe inquisitively.

"It's nothing, Charlotte. Really," Miss Hope said, still chuckling. "But you can go now if you like. I'll be closing soon."

Charlotte brightened. "You wouldn't mind?"

"Of course not. Run along now. But please try to be on time in the morning."

The girl blushed—Doc gathered that she must have had an interesting reason for whatever tardiness they were talking about—and quickly disappeared. Within seconds he heard the slam of a back door.

"You said you will be closing, Miss Hope?"

"Yes."

"If you have no other engagements, would you honor me with your presence at supper?"

"Oh my," she said. "Gallant as well as handsome. Are you trying to turn my head, sir?"

"Uh, yes. Actually." He smiled at her.

She laughed again. "Then consider it done, sir." She winked at him and went to the front door. She turned the lock, pulled down the shade over the door window, and turned a hand-lettered sign around to display CLOSED toward the street.

"That certainly took long enough," he said.

"The pressures of business, Mr. Weatherbee. Can you forgive me?"

"I'll try."

"As for your invitation to supper, sir. Did you have a particular place in mind?"

"I don't know your town," he said. "Do you have a suggestion?"

She pretended to think for a moment. "The very finest, I believe. If you care for rib roast."

"That sounds fine."

"But I warn you, sir, a rib roast takes a long time to cook. And this one is not in the oven yet."

Doc smiled at her, and Miss Hope led the way into the back of the store where her living quarters were.

CHAPTER NINETEEN

Faith stepped out of her underthings, hooked a toe under them, and kicked them toward the needlepoint-covered straight chair in the corner. She missed, but neither she nor Doc minded.

Doc was already naked, lying stretched out on top of the coverlet on her bed. He had both pillows propped behind his head and was enjoying the view inside the small bedroom.

Faith seemed to be enjoying the display as well. Certainly she had much to be proud of.

She was tall and lean. Her breasts were set high on her torso and were firm, standing tall and proud away from the smooth curves of her belly and hips.

"Are you *sure* you don't mind waiting for dinner?" she teased.

"Perhaps there's something else I could eat," he suggested. "Just a little something to hold me over."

She laughed and came to him. She moved slowly, sinuously. She reached up and pulled some pins from her hair, allowing it to fall in a rich, flowing spill over her shoulders. She tossed her head and sat lightly on the edge of the bed. Her hands went to his chest, the nails trailing and tickling their way down toward his crotch.

"Come to think of it," she said, "I'm a little hungry myself."

Doc cupped her right breast in his hand and kneaded the warm, soft, sensitive flesh. He ran his thumb lightly over an erect nipple, and Faith's breath quickened. Her flesh was silken, and she was very pale.

Her head dipped low as she gently hefted his balls. She ran her tongue over the head of his shaft, then nipped at him carefully with her teeth. Just enough to tantalize, not so much as to hurt.

Doc shifted over to make room for her and pulled her onto the bed beside him. She lay next to him, head to crotch, offering herself to him in several ways at once.

He felt the moist heat as her lips slid around him and she began to suck lightly on him, pulling him inside her mouth and continuing to toy with his balls with both hands.

It was a favor that rightfully should be returned. Faith's thighs parted as he leaned to her. She had a delightfully clean, lightly scented odor and a taste that was pleasant.

He nibbled at her for a moment, then began to stroke her tiny, fleshy button with the tip of his tongue. She wriggled her hips, pressing herself against him, and sucked harder.

"There's no hurry," he whispered. "Take your time and enjoy it."

"I am," she mumbled around the head of his cock. "I am."

"Good."

He went back to what he had been doing. Very slowly. Pausing now and then, giving her time to build, not wanting her to reach her climax too quickly.

Faith rolled partially under him, pressing her hands against his rump to pull him along with her and keep him in her warm, eager mouth.

Pushing and then pulling, she guided him, urging him to take up the stroking, giving him an unspoken permission—insisting on it, in fact—to drive deeper into her while she continued to suck on him.

Doc was reluctant at first, unwilling to hurt her, but she continued to urge him on. Gradually he allowed himself more and harder movement, drawing back until her lips contacted only the tip of his cock, then shoving forward, deeper each time, until he could feel the constriction at the upper end of her throat, finally driving on through until he had plunged into her as deep as he could go.

Faith rolled her head back to make a clear, straight passage for his entry and urged him on, using one hand to pull him into her throat, using the other to fondle and caress his balls.

Within moments he could feel the taut, sweet rise of pressure deep in his groin, and he was close to exploding inside her throat.

But there was no hurry. And he wanted to take his time with this lovely, delightful woman. He wanted to enjoy her most thoroughly.

He paused, rigid, where he was and willed himself to subside. At that moment he was deep inside her. Faith seemed to know what he was doing, what he wanted. But her mood was playful, and she seemed to want the taste of him on her tongue. She began to hum, the vibrations of it sending shivers of raw pleasure through his cock and his balls and deep inside his stomach, and at the same time she began to rock forward and back, keeping him always deep inside her throat, moving only a fraction of an inch at a time.

A fraction of an inch each time but more than enough to destroy the delicate balance he had created.

With a groan that was half exasperation and half ecstasy, he erupted, spilling into her in a long, spurting series of gushes.

He could feel the rippling contractions of her laughter in the flat of her belly even as she pressed her lips tight around the base of his shaft to slow and to heighten the pleasure she was giving him.

She drained him greedily and seemed quite proud of herself when finally she released him.

"Your turn now," he said.

"Good," she responded, not at all shy or reluctant about accepting pleasure from him, just as she had not been at all reluctant to give a similiar pleasure.

She opened herself to him and quickly reached her own release with a cry of joy.

They lay side by side like that for several minutes to allow the senses time to recuperate, then Faith pulled away from him and left the bed.

"You don't think you're done, do you?" he asked.

"I should hope *not*, sir. But I thought you might like this while you rest up for the real thing." She smiled and handed him one of his own Old Virginia cheroots, a box of matches, and a cracked saucer that was being pressed into service as an ashtray.

She rested the saucer on his bare chest, plumped the pillows behind his head, and then struck a match and held it for him to light the cheroot.

"Now that," he said, "is the absolute definition of a *good* woman."

She laughed and padded barefoot and naked out of the bedroom. When she returned she held two small snifters of brandy.

"The roast still has quite a while to cook before it will be ready," she said.

Doc smiled his approval at the delay.

Faith sat on the edge of the bed to drink her brandy. When Doc was done with his and had extinguished his cheroot she took both glasses and the saucer and set them aside.

"Time enough?" she asked.

"Mmmm."

She came into his arms, pressing the twin mounds of her breasts against his chest. She raised herself over him and poised there, allowing first the tip ends of her hair and then the warm weight of her nipples to brush lightly over his chest.

"Nice," he murmured.

"Rather."

He slid his arm around her narrow waist and pressed her down onto the bed at his side. He came to his knees, and Faith opened herself to him, reaching between their bodies to find and guide him.

He was erect again, ready for her. She was already damp and receptive. There was no need this time for preparations.

He lowered himself to her, enjoying the warm, gentle slide into the depths of her body. She was tighter that he had any right to expect. To have become so accomplished she must have had many lovers before him, but she was still as tight as a girl.

She raised her hips to meet him and locked her legs and her arms tight around him as he pressed down until his weight was riding against her pelvic bones.

Faith sighed and began to nibble lightly at his throat as he pumped in and out with long, slow strokes.

"Wait just a minute. Help me."

"All right."

He did as she asked, halting for a moment while Faith changed position so that her legs were held close together, extended high and held between his chest and hers. The new angle gave him an extraordinary degree of penetration when he pushed into her again.

Faith smiled. "Yes. Slowly now, please. Give me a moment to take it all. Oh!"

He could feel the head of his cock bumping rather rudely into some hard, bulging organ deep inside her body. He stopped when Faith stiffened for a moment in pain, then allowed her to guide him deeper once again.

She sighed. "Yes, like that. All of it now. But slowly. We wouldn't want that to happen again. Yes. Yes. Mmmm, lovely."

She urged him on in a low, soothing voice, guiding with hands and words alike, until he was pressing all the way into her.

She laughed. "I think you're at the throat again. But from the other direction this time."

It almost felt like it to him too.

"Now hard if you please. Let yourself go. As hard and as fast as you can."

He complied, pumping and bucking fiercely, driving into her like a battering ram. His weight was taken on the backs of her upraised thighs, though, and could not hurt her. He had no reason to hold anything back, and he did not.

He plunged and slammed into her soft, warm flesh, and Faith writhed and cried out, urging him to more and wilder exertions as she was filled so fully she might have been split apart.

She began a low, keening cry, grunting with effort of her own at each lunging thrust, accepting him, meeting him, demanding more and more of him.

The wordless sound continued, rising in pitch, until with a shriek she climaxed.

The rippling contractions of her sex around his shaft were the final touch to Doc's rising pleasure, and he felt the rush of hot fluids spill out of his balls and flow madly through his cock to spit deep inside her body.

With a grunt of final effort he held himself deep within her until the last drop had been expended.

Then, relaxing almost to the point of collapse, he pulled away.

He flopped down at her side and put an arm around her shoulders, pulling her to him. He was exhausted, satiated. And very, very pleased.

Faith began to slowly cover the side of his chest with soft, languid kisses.

"Did you know," she sid, "that I never, *ever* am able to make it that way. But I did with you, you dear and wonderful man."

"No," he said slowly, "I can't say that I heard anything about that on the streets of town."

"Well, sir, tomorrow you might. Because I feel so good right now that I just may dash out into the street and begin shouting it for everyone to hear. And then they shall all know what a truly shameless thing I am."

"I can think of better things for us to do than run naked in the streets," Doc said.

"Can you really?"

"Uh huh. But first you'll have to feed me."

"Promise?"

"Uh huh."

With a quick, dazzling grin she pulled away from him

and bounced to her feet beside the bed. She pushed her backside out toward him and gave it a wiggle, then ran out to the kitchen.

Fetching, Doc thought. Damned well fetching. He smiled and reached for another cheroot and the cracked saucer.

From the kitchen he could hear the clatter of plates and silverware as a table was hurriedly set and then the slam of the oven door.

The heady scent of rare roast beef lured him out through the door to where Faith was getting a meal on the table with remarkable speed and efficiency.

CHAPTER TWENTY

"I still say there's better'n a damn good chance that those boys are buried somewhere back on the Timmons place," Raider said. "But we'll pay hell proving it now." He shook his head and spit a piece of gristle into the fire. That, at least, was one good thing that had come of the fight with Ralph. Now that the damned Timmons outfit knew they were around there was no harm in shooting some meat and building a fire. Raider appreciated the opportunity to have coffee even more than he did the fresh venison provided by a whitetail they had busted out of the brush.

"Are we going back?" Charlie asked. He sounded ready, even though Raider had already patiently explained several times over that a return now was much too likely to lead to gunplay. And as Raider had also tried to explain, you don't shoot a man because of what you suspect. Only on account of what you know for damn sure.

"No, damn it, we're not going back."

"But . . ."

"We'll work it out," Raider snapped. He was beginning to lose patience with this kid. "Besides, for all we know, something could have happened south of here. Our next stop will be down at that next town. What'd you say it was again?"

"Three Trees."

"You ever been there?"

Charlie shook his head. "We passed it by comin' up, and o' course I wasn't with them goin' back. So I never been there."

"Then there won't be any pissed-off daddies waiting for you with a shotgun," Raider said. He reached for the coffeepot and refilled his cup.

"Rade!" Charlie protested.

"Hell, I was just funning you some. Don't get in an uproar about it."

The Timmons outfit knew they were still in the country, but they didn't know exactly where. As soon as they were done with the evening meal and Charlie was washing up, Raider kicked the fire apart and smothered the coals with dirt. They moved the camp another mile south before they bedded down. With no legal ground to stand on, Raider wanted no unnecessary disputes with Maxwell Timmons or his riders.

Early in the morning they ate quickly, saddled up, and headed down toward Three Trees.

There was no road to follow, but the short-cropped grass and many droppings that had been left behind by the passing Boatwright herd gave them a broad trail to follow in the general direction. Late in the afternoon Charlie pointed out a creek bed running in from the west.

"Accordin' to what Mr. Boatwright said on the way up, that town should be over there somewhere."

"And you say they intended to stop there on their way back?"

"That's what they said, but I don't know if they ever done it."

"Well, we're fixing to find out, boy." Raider turned his horse up the tiny creek.

The little creek was an odd one, shallow as they all would be expected to be but also with a narrow, closely defined bed and only a few clumps of willow growing along the banks. It had to be spring fed, Raider decided, with very little surrounding slopes to feed it, or the strong waters at spring melt time would have gouged a bed many times wider and deeper than this puny thing.

They followed it for several miles, twisting and turning, and eventually came to a hollow among the surrounding hills with a few weathered buildings set more or less in a circle.

"Three Trees, I presume," Raider said. "But if it was named for three actual trees, looks like some sonuvabitch has cut them all for firewood." There was nothing growing anywhere in sight that was taller than a blade of grass.

Charlie laughed and bumped his horse into a lope.

"Mind what I told you, boy," Raider called after him. "You let me do all the asking."

"Yes, sir," the kid floated over his shoulder. Then he dug his spurs into the sides of his tired horse and thundered the rest of the way into Three Trees. Raider followed behind at a calmer pace.

By the time Raider tied his horse in front of the town's only saloon and went inside, young Krepp was already on his second whiskey.

"... fastest man with a gun there's ever been," the kid was saying to an equally young but much rougher-looking cowhand beside him.

"Hi," Charlie said when Raider came inside. He sounded as pleased to see the Pinkerton operative as if they had been separated for days not minutes. "I was just telling my friend here about you, Rade."

"That's him, is it?" the other youngster asked.

"Yeah. Rade and me, we're saddle pards. Ain't we, Rade?" Without waiting for an answer he turned and began yelling to the bartender, even though the man was only a few paces distant. "C'mon now, hurry up. My pard's here and I know he's thirsty. Set him up, mister. On me."

The other youngster at the bar didn't seem to share Krepp's excitement about the arrival of the Pinkerton man. He turned his back to the bar and propped both elbows on it, then gave Raider a cold looking over.

"So you're the fastest man with a gun that ever lived, huh?" His voice had a hint of challenge in it.

Raider smiled at the youngster and accepted the shot glass the barman set in front of him. "I think Charlie's been gilding the lily a mite," he said pleasantly. "And I expect any man could call me a liar an' be fair about it if I was to make that claim for myself, son."

Raider's words had been deliberately mild. Hell, he didn't want to have any trouble with this kid he had never seen before and held nothing against. But the damned kid seemed to have heard none of that. At least the only part he responded to was Raider's final word.

He bristled and straightened. His hand hung like a hook over the butt of the revolver at his belt. "Who the fuck d'you think you're calling 'son'? You ain't my daddy, and you got no right to tell me *nothing*, mister."

Raider sighed. He felt weary all of a sudden. Damn it, between Charlie and this young fool he had so quick-like linked up with, it threatened to make Raider feel old and all bent by the weight of experience. And that was a natural fact.

"All right," Raider said. "In that case, boy, I'll remember not to tell you anything." He faced the bar and took a drink of the whiskey. It was not particularly good, but he had tasted worse. "Thanks for the drink, Charlie," he muttered. "But I sure as hell wish you'd learn to keep your mouth shut."

"Rade, you know I never meant—"

"Hey," the other youngster barked in a loud, hostile tone of voice, interrupting.

"You want something, boy?" Almost reluctantly, Raider turned. The kid had moved away from the bar onto the open floor between it and the door so that there was no longer anyone standing between them.

"Yeah. I want to know if you ever heard of a man called Jack Forrest." The kid was so tense he looked ready to fly apart, and the hand that he held hovering just over the grips of his revolver was shaking slightly.

Raider pretended to think about that. After a moment he pursed his lips and said, "No-o-o-o, don't think I have, boy. I've heard of Jack Ketchum and Jack Frost, jack oak and jackknife and jack off. But I don't reckon I've ever heard of this Jack Forrest."

"Well, you're *gonna* hear about him," the kid said. "You and everybody else in the whole damn country. 'Cause Jack Forrest *is* the fastest man with a gun that's ever been. And I don't care what you or your buddy here says."

"I take it you'd be Jack Forrest?" Raider asked.

"Damn right I am, mister."

"And you're the fastest man with a gun there ever was, huh?"

"You'd better believe it."

"Your buddies all tell you that, do they?"

"That's right, mister. It's mighty well known around here."

"Then I'm real glad you told me, Jack, or I might've made the mistake of thinking I could draw against the fastest man in the country." Raider turned back to the bar and picked up his drink. He was still willing to let it go. Shit, killing a kid like Forrest would be about on a level with clubbing hogs in the head at butchering time. And he had never gotten any thrill out of that.

"You fucking coward."

Raider ignored him, although that was getting more and more difficult to do.

Raider really believed it still would have been all right. Some of the other men in the place were moving toward Forrest, saying something to him, likely trying to get him to quit showing his ass like he'd been.

But then Charlie had to turn around and open his mouth too.

"You're nothing but a pissant shitkicker that isn't fit to draw against a real man like my pal Rade here. Hell, Forrest, I can take you my own self."

The men who had been approaching Forrest quite sensibly backed away again.

Raider turned and before Krepp knew what he was up to had snaked Charlie's gun out of the thing he called a holster. Raider took the old pistol away from him and shoved it behind his own belt, hoping while he did so that the ornery contraption wouldn't choose that moment to discharge.

"Rade!" Charlie protested. "Gimme my gun back. I can take that bastard. You know I can."

"Yeah, mister. Let me have him. It'd be a fair fight."

"Uh huh," Raider said. "If you give him a half hour head start it'd be a fair fight." He shook his head. "Jesus."

"He won't help you none, mister. An' neither will I. Now are you gonna draw or are you so chickenshit you'll turn tail and slink out of here like the coward you are?"

"Son, you're commencing to piss me off," Raider said. "And you don't want to do that. You really don't."

"I told you not to call me that, you son of a bitch. Now go for your gun, or I'll shoot you down like the dog you are. I swear it. I will."

Forrest had worked himself into a first-class lather. He was so tight he was quivering, and he had dropped down into what he likely thought was a "real" gunfighter's crouch.

If the little bastard had been a few steps closer Raider would have taken his gun away too and then used the damned thing to spank him with. There ought to be a fucking law, Raider thought. They just ought to keep guns out of the hands of young assholes like Krepp and Forrest.

But the little shit was not that close, and he damn sure acted like he meant every word he said.

Even with all the insults, though, even with the thoroughgoing prick that this Jack Forrest was, Raider still would have preferred being able to avoid killing him. He decided to give it one last try.

"Forrest, how many men have you killed in your time? I don't mean contests, neither. I don't mean the sort of thing where two of you square off to an empty whiskey bottle or something like that. I mean how many men have you actually faced when they were trying to put a bullet in your guts?"

Forrest's angry expression and his refusal to answer were answer enough.

"I thought so," Raider said. "Now listen to me—"

His intention was purely honorable. He wanted to give the young fool some advice, the sort of wisdom a Dutch uncle might impart. But the kid didn't give him time for that. Forrest interrupted with a barked, "Now!" and went for his gun.

The kid was fast. Raider had to give him that much. His buddies hadn't been lying to him when they told him he was quick with a gun.

But hell, a lot of men are quick with a gun. A lot of men could probably outdraw Raider—or Weatherbee or half a dozen other men Raider could have named out of hand— and had time left over to roll a smoke and drink a cup of coffee.

The difference was that most of those blazingly fast show-offs did their draws in front of a mirror or in the sort of competition where the loser's only penalty is having to pay for a round of drinks.

The difference was that Raider's experience was in drawing against other men whose intention was to plant a hot slug in his belly or to split his head open like a ripe melon.

Jack Forrest had never before faced another man with a loaded gun and serious intentions.

The kid's hand flashed, and the barrel of his Colt jumped out of the leather like it had a life of its own.

But this was the real thing, and the kid was understandably nervous.

His thumb hooked the hammer back before the barrel had cleared the holster, just the way it was supposed to be done, and before the revolver came level his grip was already shifting to the trigger, applying pressure.

It was a picture-perfect fast draw, just the way it was supposed to be done.

Except for one little thing.

In his nervousness, Forrest was yanking on the trigger too fast, reaching too much for speed and paying no attention whatsoever to accuracy.

And just like the man said, fast noises never hurt a whole hell of a lot.

Raider watched with an almost calm detachment as Forrest blew the shit out of the floor between them.

He was almost unaware that his own muscle responses

had taken over. As soon as Forrest's hand had moved, so had Raider's.

And Raider was *not* looking for extra speed; he was *not* distracted by nervousness; if anything he was willing himself to hold back.

Before Jack Forrest's Colt barked, before the kid's bullet gouged a splintery hole in the softwood floor of the saloon, Raider's barrel was lined up on the kid's belt buckle and the last ounces of pressure were being applied to the trigger of the Remington.

Raider realized barely in time and tried to throw his shot wide.

The little son of a bitch was trying to make a name for himself, but even so Raider didn't want to kill him.

He jerked his wrist at the last possible instant, trying to send his shot wide so the kid wouldn't die so foolishly.

Forrest's Colt jumped in recoil as the kid was still occupied with trying to bring it on line, and Raider's big .45 thundered.

By the sheerest chance—Raider damn sure didn't intend it—the slug he had meant to send burning harmlessly past Jack Forrest's ribs crunched into the frame of Forrest's revolver. It wasn't the sort of shot anyone would have tried to make—or could possibly have made—on purpose, but by pure accident the bullet hit the back of the Colt's frame, ripped on through the hammer, and sent pieces of tempered steel hammer and soft, torn lead into Forrest's gun hand.

Forrest screamed, and his shattered revolver went flying across the room. He grabbed his right hand in his left and bent over in agony with blood coursing off his fingertips.

"God A'mighty," someone breathed. "He went an' shot the gun right outta that boy's hand."

Charlie Krepp looked as proud as if he had done the shooting himself.

Obviously the people in the place thought the shooting had been on purpose.

Damn fools, Raider muttered to himself.

One thing for sure, though. The fastest "man" with a

gun this country had ever seen would never again pull a weapon on anyone.

Jack Forrest's right hand was shattered and useless. And it likely always would be.

Forrest looked at Raider with shocked disbelief on his young face. He tried to say something but could not. Tears came to his eyes and began to flow down his cheeks. Humiliated and in pain, the youngster turned and ran out of the saloon into the falling darkness.

Raider looked at Krepp and then at the others in the now silent room with distaste. They were gathering around him with congratulations on their lips, some of them looking at him in awe, others with raw adulation. He felt disgusted rather than pleased.

Piss on them. He could ask his questions about the Boatwright crowd later. He turned and stalked out of the place, with an excited Charlie Krepp tagging along at his heels.

CHAPTER TWENTY-ONE

"Are you sure of that?"

The bellboy, young and very eager to please, looked down first at the note he held in his hand and then at the turnip-shaped watch he was so self-importantly carrying. "Yes, sir, I'm real sure. I was supposed to wake you at 6:15 an' tell you to meet the lady in her room at 6:45 for breakfast. Mr. Nathan took the request last night an' wrote it all down for me an' told me to be sure an' not forget this morning." He held the note so Weatherbee could read it for himself if he chose.

The boy had been right on the button about the time, too. Doc had heard him stop outside his room door several minutes before the appointed moment of 6:15. He must have been standing there with the watch in his hand waiting for the exact stroke of the minute before he knocked.

"All right," Doc said. "Thanks." He tipped the boy a dime and closed the door on the relieved bellboy.

It was damn sure a curious thing, though. Angela Boatwright wanted him to call for her at her room at 6:45? She had not wanted to speak to him, much less take a meal with him, in days. And now she wanted him to call for her and take her to breakfast?

Strange indeed, Doc thought.

He glanced at his own watch to make sure he had plenty of time, then gathered up his travel case and went down the hall to the bathing room to shave and take his morning crap, then returned and finished dressing.

By the time he was ready he still had not arrived at any reasonable cause for a change of heart by Angela Boatwright. Still, he was supposed to do everything he could to please the woman—although it was certain that Allan Pinkerton could not know the utter impossibility of that assignment—and he would do what he could.

He did take the precaution, though, of slipping his Colt .38 into his pocket before he went to make his obligatory call on the lady.

His knock on her hotel room door was answered by a spoken "come." With a shrug he twisted the knob and let himself into the room, the very best room Spearfish had to offer.

Inside, he had to hide the grin of comprehension that wanted to mar the occasion for the woman.

Mrs. Boatwright was punishing him, by Jove.

The fool woman was trying to show him what he was missing.

Angela was still abed, lying back against a pair of plump pillows with the sheet not quite high enough to cover those pale monuments that rode on her chest, her hair a silky, jet spill across the white of the pillowcases.

And at her side, snoring, was one of the biggest, roughest, homeliest men Weatherbee had ever seen.

Doc could smell the sweat of the crude fellow all the way across the large room, and the portions of him that Doc could see looked positively gritty with long unwashed dirt.

Big as he was, though, with muscles that probably corded and rippled when he moved, the poor fellow looked like he had spent his childhood being kicked in the face by a long and energetic succession of mules.

Angela Boatwright looked smug as hell at the thought of what Doc was seeing in her bed. She feigned surprise, if not very convincingly, and said, "Gracious, is it that time already, Mr. Weatherbee?"

"Uh huh," Doc said pleasantly. "You wanted me to take you down to breakfast?"

"Please." Angela swept the sheet back, exposing herself to him fully, and got out of bed.

Doc had to admit that she was a screaming beauty, with a figure that would make an octogenarian do handstands, a study in contrasts between her pale, unmarred flesh and the gleaming black hair. Hair that was entirely visible in several different places, he noticed.

Had it not been for Faith's company the night before, he likely would have been turning some handstands himself right now. But as it was he was able to take the performance comfortably enough.

Angela gave him an eyeful and was in no hurry to turn and pick up her robe.

Doc's response was probably not quite what Mrs. Boatwright had had in mind when she set it up. Instead of being overcome by remorseful lust at the sight of what he himself had passed up, Doc felt a strong pang of sorrow for John Boatwright. He had never met the man, but Allan certainly thought well of him. And no man deserves a wife like the fair Angela.

Smiling, Doc ignored the woman and crossed the room to the man's side of the bed. He shook the fellow by the shoulder. It took several attempts to bring him around to some measure of wakefulness.

The man's snoring ceased, then he snorted loudly and opened one eye.

"Good morning," Doc said cheerfully. "Mrs. Boatwright and I are going down to breakfast. You'll join us, won't you."

"Huh?" The lone, confused word sounded like it came from the bottom of a pit.

"I asked—"

"I heard you. Shit, I ain't deaf." The man looked from Doc to Angela and back again. He seemed thoroughly disoriented and at a loss as to what he should do next. Big as he was he also looked frightened at being caught in the bed of another man. Just what other man he probably did not know, although this elegantly dressed gentleman standing over his bed was not acting like a wronged husband.

Eventually he gave up thinking—probably a difficult process for him, Doc thought—and asked, "What the hell, lady?"

Before Angela had a chance to answer, Doc spoke for her. "Really, my good man, we would be delighted if you could join us for breakfast." Doc extended a hand. "My name is Weatherbee. And yours, sir?"

The man looked half fearfully from the outstretched hand to Angela and back again. He swallowed hard and pulled the sheet up under his chin. After a moment he stuck his hand out from under the covers and hesitantly shook. "They, uh, everybody calls me Bull." He said it shyly.

"Well, it's a pleasure to meet you, Bull." Doc smiled at him.

The big man seemed relieved. "You, uh, don' mind if I get dressed now?"

"Please do."

Bull crawled out of the bed and stood. When he did he towered over Doc, who was no small man himself.

Bull's shoulders were wide enough that he could have been yoked and put into an ox team, and his chest and massive, hairy thighs were sized to match. A rank, primal odor filled the air around him. He was rather well named, Doc thought.

Yet in spite of his massive size in all other aspects, the shriveled thing that dangled between his thighs was small enough to be buried in the tangle of his pubic hair.

Doc had to suppress another grin. Poor Mrs. Boatwright had not gotten quite everything she'd bargained for when she picked up Bull.

And Doc had absolutely no doubts about who had picked up whom last night. Shy, ignorant Bull would never have dreamed of speaking to a woman like Mrs. Boatwright, much less actually propositioning her, without some rawly blatant encouragement. In fact, Doc suspected, Angela probably had to put a ring in the poor man's nose and drag

him up the stairs by main strength. He turned his head away
to hide his expression from Bull. But not from Angela. The
look he got from her in return would have withered every
wildflower in a ten-mile radius if it had been unleashed
outside the hotel room walls.

Doc gave the woman a cheerful wink and got another
fiery blast from those lovely dark eyes.

Angela angrily pulled her clothes on, while Bull quickly
got into his.

Bull, of course, had considerably less to get into than
did the lady. While she was fussing and fuming over her
corset ties, he stepped into a ragged pair of trousers and a
shirt that looked like it had been in use for greasing axles
before he received it. Several buttons were missing from
the rag, and a seam under his right arm had split. Apparently
the man owned no refinements like underwear or socks. He
stuffed his big feet—hairy toes, Doc noticed—into a pair
of battered, muddy shoes, and the man was dressed.

"May I help you with those shoe buttons, Mrs. Boatwright?" Doc asked gallantly. He knelt while she sat on the
side of the rumpled, sweat-smelling bed and helped her
button her shoes.

His attitude of outward helpfulness almost to the point
of subservience was quite correctly interpreted by Angela
Boatwright for the mocking sham that it was. The woman
was furious, but there was nothing she could say or do about
it. She had made her own bed—or unmade it, to be more
accurate—and now she was forced to lie in it. She looked
like she wanted to spit.

"Shall we go down to breakfast now?" Doc asked when
she was ready. His expression was that of cheerful helpfulness, but his eyes were laughing.

He and Mrs. Boatwright knew quite well what the opinion of the other hotel patrons would be when they saw the
lady being squired by Bull, who had no idea of the things
that were going on in this room nor of the whispers that
would fly around the hotel very shortly.

Angela gave Doc a look that would have dropped a weak-hearted man, then raised her chin and set her lips in a thin, prim line. "Thank you, Mr. Weatherbee. I am quite ready now."

Doc was, he had to admit, surprised. He had expected her to beg off. After all, any woman can conjure up a headache without notice. But she was going to ride with it. He supposed he would have to give her some credit for that much, anyway.

Doc offered Mrs. Boatwright his elbow, and Bull, aping him, did the same, and the three of them went down to breakfast.

Weatherbee could hardly remember when he had enjoyed a meal more.

CHAPTER TWENTY-TWO

It didn't take long for Raider to question everyone who lived in or near Three Trees. He saved going back to the saloon for last, thinking that there he could ask about the Boatwright crew not only of the proprieter but also of most of the men who lived in the country surrounding the tiny town.

Charlie Krepp followed Raider on his rounds of conversation and for once kept mostly quiet except for joyful comments about Raider's feat of shooting the gun out of Jack Forrest's hand. And those dried up when Raider finally got tired of the kid's nattering and snapped at him.

After that Charlie's wounded sighs were a little tiresome, but they were easier to take than the chatter had been.

They had supper at the town's lone greasy spoon eatery, which did Raider's digestion no particular good, and then drifted back to the saloon. There was a sudden hush when Raider entered the place, quickly followed by a buzz of whispering. Apparently his reputation was better established here than he could ever want. Jack Forrest probably would have loved it. Raider did not.

"You don't need me for anything, do you, Rade?" Charlie asked when they each had a beer in hand.

Raider shook his head.

"I'm gonna go over and sit in on that card game, then.

If you need anything, though, I'll be glad to—"

"No, Charlie. It's all right."

"But if you need me—"

"I know," Raider said patiently. "If I need you for anything, I'll ask."

"Okay." Charlie grinned at him and went to join a group of men playing stud poker at one of the few tables in the place.

Raider took a swallow of his beer, which tasted better than the whiskey had earlier, and motioned for the barman to join him.

"Yeah? Uh, you aren't going to cause any trouble in here, are you?"

"I sure as shit hope not."

"Yeah, well, I know that business earlier wasn't your fault an' all that, but—"

"No trouble," Raider assured him. "I just wanted to ask if you've seen some men around here. Several weeks back it would've been now."

The barman gave him a suspicious look.

"No trouble. I already told you that. These men are missing, and the boss's wife has hired Pinkertons to find them." He knew better than to mention anything about a quarter of a million dollars being missing along with the men. Word about that would get results but not exactly the kind that Pinkertons wanted. Hell, word about that would start riots, and there wouldn't be a half a dozen men left in their homes by the break of day tomorrow. The whole damned countryside would be out looking for the money, with or without John Boatwright and his men.

"You're a Pink?"

"Uh huh."

The bartender looked relieved. Pinkerton operatives were not known for depopulating small towns. Apparently the man had had some doubts. Now, though, he relaxed and refilled Raider's mug free of charge. "Who is it you're looking for?"

"The boss's name is Boatwright. John Boatwright. He has a riding crew with him. Or did when he left Maxwell

Timmons's place a while back." Raider named the rest of the men and added descriptions of Boatwright, his men, and of the horses they had been riding.

"Shit, man, there hasn't been a crew passing through here since the last time Timmons bought cows. But no, I ain't seen nothing of that crowd. I'd sure remember if I had, that many boys buying and everything."

Raider grunted and took a swallow of the beer. The barman certainly sounded and acted open and honest about it. He seemed perfectly at ease, although Raider watched both his eyes and his hands for any display of untoward nervousness.

"You know Timmons, then?" Raider prompted.

"Hell, yes. Hard not to know of him if you live in this part of the country. He has a helluva big spread, and he's been buying cattle to stock it. If this fella . . . what'd you say his name was?"

"Boatwright."

"Yeah, well, if this Boatwright brought a herd up too, that's the second delivery this summer that I know about. And Timmons had some brought in last fall. All of them aside from what he bought range delivery when he took over the place."

Raider's interest was piqued. The purchase of that many cattle would require one hell of a lot of capital. Or one hell of a lot of theft. Even if the other herds had been considerably smaller than John Boatwright's nine thousand head, it would still add up to a pile of money to pay for all those bovines.

"Timmons must have a lot of land to carry that many cattle," Raider prompted. "And a lot of money to pay for them."

"Hell, I reckon," the bartender said. "The man's got grass from here to next week. And money? Shit, I reckon."

Raider shook his head admiringly. "Kind of makes a man wonder how some of us can be so broke and others be so lucky, don't it?"

"Huh. Luck hadn't nothing to do with it," the bartender said.

"How's that?"

"You mean you never heard of him before?"

"No, I can't say that I have."

"Jesus, where've you been? And you a Pink, too." The bartender shook his head in disbelief.

"So who is he?"

"Man, you never heard of Old Max beer? That's some of it you got in your hand right now, mister."

Raider shrugged. "I've heard of it, sure. Everybody has."

"Damn right everybody has. Biggest brewery in Milwaukee, or so they say."

"Old Max? As in Maxwell Timmons?" Raider asked. The light was beginning to dawn.

"Damn straight. Old Max was named for old Max Timmons Senior, though. Young Maxwell—but don't let him hear you call him that now—inherited the brewery from his father when the old man died a couple years ago. Lock, stock, and a shitpot load of barrels, and all of them filled with beer."

Raider grunted. His theory about the counterfeiting all of a sudden was not looking so good.

"The way I hear it, the family was rich as hell. Money by the carload, practically owned Wisconsin. And that was just to start with. But young Maxwell, the one we got out here now, he'd always had this bug in his bonnet that he wanted to be a cowboy. Or some such shit from back when he was a kid. So after his daddy died and left him all that money, he decided he just couldn't stand it anymore. He was gonna pick up his family and move west. Set himself up the biggest, grandest damn spread anywhere. They say he even went down to Texas and tried to buy out Cap'n King but they didn't have the proper respect for him or something down there, laughed in his face is what I'd suspect if the story's true, so he up and came north, just as far away from Texas and those King Ranch people as he could get, and vowed he'd build a ranch that'd make theirs look like a penny-ante outfit.

"Went and sold off the brewery to some German family—they say they're gonna keep the brewery, which is a damn good one, and the recipe too, but that they're going to change the name soon—and he come on out here. I got no idea how much a brewery like that would have brought in, but I hear it was all cash money. And that's on top of what he already had salted away in half the banks in this country and a hell of a lot of banks in other places." The bartender shook his head. "I sure as hell hope they keep the same distributor when they go to changing things around, because I sure like the fella I've been dealing with."

"I'll be damned," Raider muttered.

Counterfeiting? It sounded like Maxwell Timmons didn't *need* a printing press of his own. He already had the keys to the damned mint.

Raider took another swallow of his beer and almost choked on it when another thought came to him.

Those homely, unpretentious women back at the Timmons place. Crystal, with her glasses and her big tits. And her mother, who was so hot to get Raider interested in her daughter that she might have suggested that nighttime visit.

Shee-it!

He wondered if he would have acted any different back there if he had known just how rich the damn girl's daddy was.

He thought about that some. And the simple truth was that he didn't know.

He knew what he would *like* to be able to claim about it. But in all honesty he simply was not sure.

Jesus!

CHAPTER TWENTY-THREE

He heard the clatter of a chair, followed by a sudden silence in the crowded saloon. Raider turned quickly, his hand automatically moving toward the grips of the Remington.

He relaxed when he saw the pale, static expression of the man at the card table. It was one of the people Charlie had been playing stud with. The fellow had simply gotten up from the table too fast or something. He gave Raider a worried look, then, when Raider removed his hand from his revolver, went back to picking up his money from the table. His chair had fallen over behind him. Apparently that was all there was to it. Raider relaxed, and so did the unhappy poker player.

He did look unhappy, Raider noticed. Probably he had lost.

Charlie, on the other hand, looked as content as a clam. He had a stack of coins in front of him that looked more yellow than silver, so he must have been doing well.

Raider drifted over beside him. "Well?"

"I sure been lucky tonight," Charlie said with a grin.

The man who had just left the table came back for a moment to bend and whisper something to another of the players.

"Yeah?" the player asked. "I mean, uh, sure, I'd like to

go with you. If these fellows wouldn't mind." Oddly he was looking at Raider when he said that, even though Raider had not been involved in the game.

Raider shrugged, and the player gathered up his money and joined the other man.

Charlie watched them go and fingered his winnings. He had said he was generally lucky with the cards. He must have been telling the truth.

"I think I'll pack it in too," Charlie said with a smile. "Can I buy you a drink, Rade?"

Raider shook his head. "That beer was enough. My stomach don't feel so good after supper. Too greasy or something."

Charlie winked at him. "I got a better idea anyhow." He went to the bar and asked the bartender, "You fellas got any loose women in Three Trees? You know the kind I mean?"

"Sure, son, you can find that kind anywhere. Even in Three Trees."

"Well?"

"Second floor, right on top of the mercantile. There's a staircase around back. It's a real quiet place, mind. They don't allow no drinking or no rowdiness."

"Thank you, sir." He turned to Raider. "My treat, Rade. Just like before."

Raider started to protest, then, looking at Charlie's delighted expression, accepted the gift that the boy was so pleased to be able to offer. "All right."

They walked the short distance to the mercantile store—anywhere in Three Trees was a short distance from anywhere else in the town—and followed an alley to the back of the place. There, as the bartender had said, was a set of stairs. There were no signs or lights visible, but then, in a town so small none would be needed; everyone would already know where to go.

Charlie led the way up the stairs and knocked loudly on the door. It was opened by a diminutive woman scaled to a size against other women the way Three Trees would match up to Kansas City or other metropolises. Raider could not see until they were inside and the light was no longer behind the tiny woman that she was an Oriental. Just what kind of Oriental he was not sure, since she did not have the flat face and the dark skin of most of the Chinese girls he had seen before. She was, in fact, quite attractive.

"Greetings, sirs," she said. Her accent was faint, as delicate as her form. Her hair and eyes were very black, her skin pale. It was mostly the almond shape of her eyes and a pronounced long-waistedness that proclaimed her racial heritage.

"We come to get laid," Charlie announced with a grin.

Subtle, Raider thought. The kid is really smooth.

"Of course, sirs." The little woman bowed them inside and accepted their hats. Raider would have balked if she had wanted their guns too—he had known places that made that demand—but she did not mention them. She then led them into a small room furnished as a parlor.

"You're the one for me," Charlie cried with joy when he saw an attractive blonde with large, drooping breasts sitting on the sofa.

Charlie grabbed the blonde around the waist and danced her around the room for a moment, then broke away long enough to hand the madam a gold coin.

"That's for me an' my pal too, you savvy, chop-chop?"

The tiny Oriental gave him a look of restrained distaste. But she accepted his money. Charlie appeared not to have noticed. He turned to grab the blonde again, and she led him away to a private room.

Raider looked questioningly around the room. There were no other customers and no other girls in sight.

Not that it was going to fall off and rot if he didn't use it tonight. And he damn sure was not going to take seconds behind Charlie Krepp with that saggy blonde.

"My apologies, sir," the little woman said. "My other employee is indisposed with her monthlies. Would you care to wait, or may I accommodate you."

"Accommodate." Raider mouthed the word carefully. "That has a nice sound to it."

"Yes, sir." The woman waited for his answer with no indication of interest. Raider did not find that particularly flattering, but then he was under no illusions about the madam's occupation either. It was the money that was important here, not the meat.

He looked at her. Certainly she was attractive enough. And he could not help remembering another Oriental, a Chinese girl, he and Doc had encountered not too long before. She'd been a pretty thing, he recalled. Her name would not come to him at the moment. But it had been old Weatherbee that that one had taken a shine to. And he had to confess to a certain amount of curiosity....

"I'd be right proud if you would, uh, accommodate me, ma'am," he said.

"Of course, sir." She bowed to him, then took him by the hand and led him to one of the back rooms. Front, actually, he corrected himself. The rooms at the "back" of the place would be over the street, since the entry was at the back of the building.

The room was small but a lot better furnished than some places he had seen. There was a bed and chair and nightstand. The nightstand held a lamp with the wick turned low, an ashtray, and a basin and pitcher set in a matching floral pattern.

The little woman helped Raider out of his clothing, then quickly slipped out of her kimono as well.

He doubted that she would reach five feet and likely was several inches short of that, but her figure was fine enough.

Small at waist and breast, very slightly full in the thighs. Pale and smooth. Her nipples were exceptionally small, hardly larger than dimes.

The most unusual thing about her was how scanty her pubic hair was. It was dark but so wispy-thin a bush that he could see the individual hairs.

She posed for him, turning around so that he could inspect her from all sides—her ass was nicely rounded, and one side of her was quite as nice as any other—then poured water into the basin.

She motioned for Raider to sit on the side of the bed while she knelt in front of him. He thought for a moment that she was offering to suck him, but instead she dipped a washcloth into the basin and used it to wash his cock and his balls. She took her time about it and was gentle but also careful to wash every part of him. Then she dried him with a small, soft towel.

When she was done with him she straddled the basin and used the same water to wash herself with every bit as much care as she had applied to him.

"Now, sir," she said when she was done. "What is your pleasure tonight?"

"Well, uh, you know."

She smiled. "Of course, sir."

She came to him. When she lay at his side she seemed even smaller than he had realized. He was pretty damned well hung. He hoped he wouldn't hurt her.

He touched her breast, placing his palm over it and cupping it gently.

The madam laughed. "I won't break, sir. I wish to please you. Use me as you wish."

Raider laughed too—at himself. He had not realized until then just how tentative he was being with her. She was a whore. She had been with a thousand men, probably. He sure wasn't going to hurt her.

He threw an arm around her and pulled her to him.

The little woman's body was cool to the touch and very soft, but there was strength in that small frame too. She rolled on top of him and straddled him, clamping strong thighs around his waist and bending to apply her tongue to his chest and nipples. The sensation of it was warm and tingly.

He took her breasts again, one in each hand, and found that they really didn't break when he kneaded and stroked them. They were small but surprisingly soft and flowed like water through his fingers when he grasped them.

The woman rubbed herself against him, grasping his shaft between the lips of her sex and rubbing up and down.

If she intended to arouse him that way she was doing just fine, even if the chore was unnecessary. He was damn well ready as it was.

"Nice, yes?" she asked.

"Nice," he agreed.

"Yes, very." She continued to rub him with the gaping pussy lips but moved slowly higher at the end of each stroke until the head of his cock was bouncing each time at her entrance.

Then, with a small shiver, she changed the angle of her hips and captured him there.

She sat up, allowing herself to slide down on him until he was inside her. Her body was hot, and either she was as ready as he was or she had prepared herself ahead of time by adding a lubricant.

With Raider trapped—but not unwillingly—inside her, she shifted position again, this time placing her feet on either side of his waist and squatting until her buttocks pressed down against his balls.

He found it mildly incredible that so small a woman could take so much into herself without discomfort. He knew damn good and well where the head of his cock should be, and if he was right about that it had to be resting now somewhere just behind her belly button.

He smiled at her.

"Nice?" she asked.

"Damn straight."

She smiled back and began to pump up and down, raising her hips from him until he almost sprang free from her, then plunging down upon him with startling force and speed. She braced her fingertips lightly against his chest and seemed quite willing for him to finish that way, with her doing all the work of their joining.

He was enjoying it, but that was not all that he wanted from her. After a few minutes he pulled her down so that she was lying on top of him, with his cock still embedded deep within her. She laughed and began to lick his chest.

Raider rolled over with her until he was on top.

"Lift your leg, please?" she asked.

He did not know exactly what she intended, but he was willing to give it a try. He did what she asked.

She pulled her leg inside of his, then had him do the same with the other leg so they ended up with his thighs outside of hers. She held her legs tightly together.

"Now try," she said.

"All right." It seemed a slightly strange idea, but he would give it a try.

He stroked in and out a few times, and a smile spread over his face. "I'll be damned," he said.

"Tight, yes?"

He laughed. "Tight as a damned virgin."

"Yes, I am a virgin," she said solemnly. Then began to laugh with him.

Damned if she didn't feel just about as tight as a first-timer though, he admitted. Not quite so deep this way, which was no drawback with one as small as this, and damn sure tight. He liked it.

He was enjoying himself right well with this odd little Oriental, and gradually he lost his concern about hurting her and was able to let go.

It was even better after that.

CHAPTER TWENTY-FOUR

Doc was getting worried. He had spent the entire late afternoon and early evening asking questions in every saloon, brothel, café, store—everything he could find open from one end of Alexander to another.

He had learned nothing about the possible whereabouts of John Boatwright and his men. But then, he had come to expect that.

The thing that was worrying him was that he had heard nothing about Raider and young Krepp either. By now Doc and Angela were far enough north that someone should have seen them. They should already have been here asking their own questions about the Boatwright crew.

Doc had really expected to run into Raider back in Belle Fourche or possibly even Spearfish, although no definite meeting place had been named.

It was always possible that Raider and Krepp could have taken a side trip that would have prevented them from meeting on the road.

But, damn it, someone surely should have seen them, talked to them, have some information about or from them.

Weatherbee was beginning to think that whatever had befallen John Boatwright and the rest of his men just might have happened to Raider and Krepp also.

Until he reached Rade's starting point at the Timmons ranch, though, there was no way for Doc to know. Either way. He could only sit and fret about it.

He grumbled a little to himself as he kicked his shoes off and loosened his tie. Ignorant, upstart, no-account fool. There were times when Doc would cheerfully separate Raider's head from his shoulders. But by damn no one *else* was going to have that privilege without Doc coming down on him like green on grass.

No one.

Doc grumped and worried some more, but there was nothing he could do about it. Not right now there wasn't.

He pulled out a cheroot and lighted it. A drink would have been good too, but he was simply too tired at the moment to go down and buy one.

Damn it.

A knock at the hotel room door interrupted his worrying. He slipped his feet back into his untied shoes and crossed the room.

The hallway was empty. He had distinctly heard someone knock, but when he opened the door there was no one there. If this was some damn-fool prankster, the kid—or twelve-foot-tall lumberjack: right at the moment it hardly seemed to matter—was going to get more out of the joke than he wanted.

Weatherbee slammed the door shut and went back toward his chair.

The knocking came again, a little louder this time.

Doc whirled, took two quick strides to the door, and snatched it open.

The hall was empty again.

Fit to bust now, Doc leaned out to glare from one end of the hall to the other. A clerkish-looking little man with spectacles and a threadbare suit came up the stairway from the lobby, saw Doc's expression, and promptly turned and went back down again.

The knocking came again, but hesitantly this time.

Doc blinked. He was standing right there in the open doorway, yet . . .

He turned. There was the connecting door to Mrs. Boat-wright's room. Not by request. The adjoining rooms were simply the only ones that had been available when they checked in. There certainly would be no other reason for them to take adjoining rooms.

But now it seemed that the woman was knocking on his door. Hardly likely, he thought, in view of the fact that they had not spoken at all, not even from necessity, since that fascinating breakfast with Moose or Horse or . . . Bull, his name had been. Bull. Doc chuckled again, just thinking about it.

So what could the woman have in mind this time? Had she brought in a troupe of traveling dwarfs and wanted Doc to watch the bunch of them perform now? He would not have put it past her.

She knocked again, and with a sigh he shut and bolted his own door, then went to open the one that connected their two rooms.

In spite of his distaste for the woman, he blinked when he saw her. "Are you all right?"

"No." It was obvious that she was not lying to him. Her hair, always so perfectly coiffed, was in tangled disarray. Her gown was rumpled, and her makeup was smeary. She looked like she had been crying.

Moreover, she looked like she had been drinking. Quite a lot.

She swayed slightly from side to side and had to reach out and grab the doorframe to brace herself and keep from falling. When she did so she damn near missed the wall.

Mrs. Boatwright was not nearly so lovely this way, but she looked more—he had to search for it for a moment before he realized—she looked more human. Always play-ing the role of the cold beauty, she now looked like a woman instead of a vision.

A tear welled in the corner of her eye, fattened until the eye could contain it no longer, and rolled down her cheek, leaving behind a wet, shiny track.

"Help me? Please?"

He had felt nothing for this woman but disgust practically

since they had met, yet Doc's response was instinctive and immediate. He moved quickly to her side, put a supporting arm around her, and led her slowly to the chair in her room.

A nearly empty bottle of excellent brandy sat on the small round table beside the chair. There were no glasses in sight. Apparently she had been nipping it straight from the bottle, which was not what he would have expected of her.

On the other hand, none of this was what he would have expected of her.

"Can I get you anything?" he asked. "Have you had anything to eat?"

She shook her head in refusal, although to which question he was not entirely sure. More tears appeared, following the paths of their predecessors.

"Have you eaten?" he asked again.

"No." The single word had a husky quaver in it.

He looked around the room, but there was no help in sight. No maids or nurses miraculously appeared.

"You should have something in your stomach," he said. "And coffee. You need some coffee."

"I can't . . . I can't go down . . . you know . . . to the restaurant."

"No," he agreed. "I'll bring something up to you."

"Would you?" She looked immeasurably grateful for his offer and clutched at his right hand with both of hers.

"Wait here," he said unnecessarily. In her present condition she was not going anywhere. Not any farther than falling out of her chair, anyway. "I'll be right back."

He stopped in his own room long enough to tie his shoes and straighten his necktie, then went down to the restaurant that was attached to the hotel. He ordered two pots of strong coffee and a tray of sandwiches and hurried back to the rooms without waiting for them to be prepared.

Angela looked confused when he returned empty-handed. He explained to her but was not sure how much of the information was sinking in. She might not have been able to focus on a word of it.

He dampened a washcloth in the basin and mopped her forehead with it, then had to return to his own room to let the bellman bring the food and coffee in. He pulled the connecting door shut when he did so, though. In spite of the pleasure he had received from making a public spectacle of her back in Spearfish, he felt no such inclination now.

Doc paid the bellman, then locked his own room door and carried the two trays into Angela's room.

He had to help her with the coffee and with the sandwiches, but by the second cup of coffee she was able to hold the cup for herself, and by the third she seemed to be in touch with reality again.

"Are you feeling better now?" he asked.

"Yes . . . no . . . I, I just feel so *ashamed*," she blurted. She began to cry again. Doc's natural response was to put an arm around her shoulders and try to comfort her.

The truth was that he was beginning to need some comforting himself. Or some cooling down at the very least. During the past few minutes the front of her gown had gaped open even more, and his response to that was embarrassing under the circumstances.

Strong drink had done a great deal to the cosmetic portions of her appearance, but it had done nothing to alter the exceptional shapeliness of her bosom.

Doc cursed himself. The woman was drunk, and she was vulnerable. Certainly she was no shrinking maiden. But even so she had the right to expect decency from him. Damn it. For probably the twentieth time in the past ten seconds, Doc forced his eyes away from the bounty on her chest and tried to look her in the eyes.

"It's going to be all right," he assured her in a gentle, soothing tone.

"But I've been so *awful*," she wailed.

There was not a lot he could say to that. It was the simple truth. She *had* been awful. She had every right to be ashamed. Still, it was good that she realized it, he thought.

She pressed her tear-streaked face into his neck and sobbed violently.

That was all right. That was even as it should be. But damn it, her movement in turning to him had caused the skirt of her dressing gown to separate too.

In addition to everything she was showing above the cloth belt of the gown, she was now exhibiting a wide expanse of sleek thigh. And a hint—he checked several times to verify the fact—of dark curly hair as well.

Doc swallowed and squeezed his eyes shut. Briefly. They came open again almost immediately, very much on their own accord. He was against it, personally, but there seemed to be parts of him that were not paying attention to what the rest of him wanted.

Her breath was hot against his neck. That was not helping matters.

Doc had an erection that was going to pop the buttons off his fly soon.

Abruptly he pulled away from her and reached for her empty coffee cup. He refilled it and shoved it blindly into her hands, then poured a second cup for himself. He needed it. Or maybe the rest of that brandy in the bottle.

He took another look. The skirt of the dressing gown was still falling away from her lap, although she seemed unaware of it. Doc wished he could say the same for himself. He was altogether *too* aware of it.

She slumped a few inches lower in the chair, holding her cup in both hands and paying attention only to it, and the front of the gown opened even more. Doc turned to face the other way and gulped down a swallow of coffee.

Perhaps . . . He turned abruptly back to face her, intending to do the honorable thing and pull that damned dressing gown together himself if he had to.

But instead of facing a slack-mouthed, drunken, conscience-stricken woman there, he caught Angela with a smug and quite thoroughly aware little smirk tickling the corners of her mouth.

Her expression went slack again immediately.

But not before he had had a chance to see what it had been when he turned.

Doc's sympathetic concern vanished as quickly as Angela's smirk just had.

"Why . . . why, you miserable bitch!" he howled.

Angela gave up the game, and the smirk returned. She threw her head back and laughed. "It worked for a while, didn't it, Weatherbee?" She laughed again. "I had your breathing going pretty fast while it lasted."

With a malicious gleam in her dark eyes she deliberately picked open the knot in her belt and dropped the remaining folds of cloth away so that she sat naked before him.

"You do like it, don't you, Weatherbee?"

Doc bristled. He fumed. He wanted to hit her, kick her, throw something at her. He didn't know exactly *what* he wanted to do to her. He wanted to do something, that was for sure.

But there was nothing he could do.

She was a woman, damn it, and he could not bring himself to hit her. He just could not.

Angela stood and let the gown fall from her fine, full body to slither across the seat of the chair and down onto the floor. She stood in front of him, showing him everything she had to offer, inviting without words, that smirking smile still playing at the corners of her mouth.

While he stared at her she parted her lips and with a provocative sensuality slowly ran the tip of her tongue over her ripe, full lips. She did it a second time while her eyes openly strayed to the bulge behind his fly.

Damn, but she was a desirable woman. Rich, ripe, and lusting.

He was angry with her, but he wanted her too. His desire for her was as strong now that he realized her deception as it had been minutes earlier when he had been feeling guilty about a near compulsion to take advantage of her.

She was a seductress, damn her, and she was good at it.

He almost wavered, almost took a step toward her.

It was Angela herself who saved him from that humiliation. And with Angela Boatwright it *would* have been humiliation. She would have seen to that.

She licked her lips again and blew a slow kiss into the air between them. "You have to have me, don't you, Weatherbee? You just have to."

Doc shook his head like a dog shaking water off itself. Have to? *Have* to? No, by damn, there were things that he did not *have* to do.

And dishonoring himself and a man named Boatwright, those were things that he did not *have* to do.

The bitch's spell was shattered, and once it was gone Doc could not remember for sure how it had been or even if. He only knew that whatever it was this woman had been charming him with no longer worked. It no longer had any effect on him. Thank God.

Doc went to her. Her eyes flared with unholy glee at the thought of her triumph. She was sure she was still in command of the situation.

He put an arm around her shoulders, placed his other hand at her waist. He bent her backward and kissed her. Her mouth was hungry, her tongue probing quickly into his mouth.

He felt her breathing quicken, much as his had so recently.

And when he was sure that she was certain of her own victory and of her chance to humiliate him, he broke the kiss and laughed loudly into her face.

"What?"

He picked her up and threw her onto the bed. She hit on her rump and bounced, almost falling off the other side. Her hair flew into a tangled mess, and she seemed confused by this new turn of events.

"Some other time, maybe," Doc said. He turned his back on her and walked out, pausing only to pluck the brandy bottle from the table as he passed it.

Angela shrieked something that he paid no attention to, and some small hard object bounced off the doorjamb as he left her room, but he didn't look back to see her or to see what she had thrown at him.

He really didn't give a damn any longer, thank goodness. He made sure the door between their rooms was bolted, then poured himself a drink.

The brandy was excellent, and he idly wondered what

she had done with the rest of the bottle when she needed a
nearly empty one as a prop for her play.

Probably poured the rest of it out, he decided. Not that
he cared. He was enjoying what she had left in the bottle.
It was more than enough for one evening.

CHAPTER TWENTY-FIVE

Charlie Krepp stood in his stirrups and peered out across the grass. He blinked, shaded his eyes with a hand, and looked again. Then he pointed. "There's something over there, Rade. A line camp or some homesteader's dugout. We could talk to them folks. They might've seen something."

"I have a better idea," Raider said. "There's a wagon coming up the road. We talk to them first. Find out if there's a stage stop or somethin' down the way where we can get a proper meal." He belched and made a sour face. "Damned if I can stand another bite of salt pork and beans, boy."

Charlie laughed. He seemed to thrive on the greasy, impossible foods that were gladly given at the isolated places along the road, but Raider did not. And Charlie seemed to have no comprehension at all of his companion's discomfort. Still, he was agreeable about going along with anything Raider said. There were certain advantages to being an idol, Raider decided.

They dropped down the hill to the thin twin tracks of what passed for a road around here and pulled their horses to a halt, waiting for the wagon to reach them. The vehicle moved along at a long trot, bouncing and swaying and boiling a fresh rise of dust in its wake. When it reached them it stopped.

"Hello, y' old sonuvabitch," Raider said.

The driver of the wagon grunted. "I was beginning to think you were dead."

"I figure to outlive you by twenty years, by damn."

"Huh. I'll kill you myself if you don't learn to send in reports and answer wires. You did get my messages, didn't you?"

Raider shrugged. "Haven't been around civilization all that much lately."

"For God's sake," Angela Boatwright snapped, "will you two stop this nonsense and find me some shade. You can talk later. Now find me some shade before I start to look like a lobster." She was holding a small, newly purchased parasol to keep the sun off her pale cheeks, but she was covered with enough dust from the road that no sunshine likely could have penetrated to her skin even without the parasol.

Doc Weatherbee gave Raider a shrug and a rare look of apology. "Is there anyplace to the north where we can pull in for the day?"

"No real civilization between here and Wolf Point. There's a settlement called Three Trees, but it ain't much. No hotel or nothing like that. Me and the kid been laying out in the brush 'most all the time since we left you."

"Wolf Point it is, then," Doc said. "We have to go there anyway."

"We do?"

"We have to talk to the town marshall there. It was all in the messages I sent you."

"I never got no messages."

"Rade, you dumb..." Doc glanced toward Mrs. Boatwright and gritted his teeth. They could go into this later. But *when* was Raider going to learn to do things by the book, the way they *ought* to be done?

"Is it far to this Wolf Point place?" Angela asked.

"Tolerable," Raider said.

She moaned and began to sway and bounce again as

Weatherbee put his team back into motion.

It took a day and a half of steady travel to return north to the Missouri, and they had to pay a tobacco-chewing ferryman three dollars to take the wagon across.

During the trip Doc filled Raider in on his lack of success to the south, and Raider more or less let Doc know about his own failures in the Timmons ranch country. He explained Timmons's wealth, neglecting to mention his early suspicions about counterfeiting.

"We're a little short on suspects, Rade," Doc told him. "The Chicago office checked out the banker in Ogallala too. They say he's honest and not nearly bold enough to do anything illegal. No sudden wealth either. Our best bet is this town marshal at Wolf Point. According to our information, they have an unidentified body up there that some cowboy found."

"Can't be one of the missing men, then. We're looking for a lot more than just the one body."

"We should investigate it anyway," Doc said primly.

"If you say so."

Charlie Krepp was subdued during the trip, quiet and attentive to Mrs. Boatwright. The woman was *not* silent. Sensing failure in the search for her husband, she complained bitterly about the loss of the money he had been carrying. But not, Doc and Raider noted, very much about the loss of the man. As before, she mentioned the missing foreman quite as much as she did her husband. Neither Doc nor Raider saw fit to elaborate on their experiences with the woman. Neither of them liked her well enough to think about her, much less comment on her.

When they reached Wolf Point they settled Mrs. Boatwright into a hotel and went to see the marshal with Charlie Krepp in tow.

"Hell, man, we buried the son of a bitch, what'd you think?" the marshal told them. "It's been a week since the body was found. And it wasn't none too fresh to begin with."

"Just the one man?" Raider asked. His opinion was that they were wasting their time asking about a single body.

"No chance there could've been others around?"

"Just the one," the marshal assured them. "The boys who found him looked around, and I went out myself to take another look. There were no other bodies."

"I hope you at least kept a photograph of the dead man's face," Doc said. "We could try to get an identification from that."

The town marshal grimaced. "No photograph."

"But surely, sir, you realize that—"

"Mr. Weatherbee. It is Weatherbee, right?"

Doc nodded.

"Maybe you don't understand what we found, but that man had been dead for a while, and he wasn't buried half deep enough to begin with. The coyotes had drug out what was left of him, and after they was done the birds and the mice had time to play. There wasn't enough left *to* photograph." The marshal got up from his desk—he had made his visitors stand while he sat in his swivel chair—and went to a file cabinet. He rummaged inside it for a moment and came out with a tan envelope that he emptied onto the desk for them.

"This is all he had on him. I kept what there was to keep, but I damn sure didn't want no pictures around."

There were few enough articles. A brass belt buckle with no markings or design on it. A bandanna, black and plain. A handful of pocket change including a five-dollar gold piece. And a Barlow knife.

Doc and Raider barely glanced at the things. Charlie Krepp moved to the desk and fingered through them.

"Thank you, Marshal," Doc said. "We appreciate your cooperation."

As they left the town marshal's office, Krepp hemmed and hawed for a moment and finally spoke up. "Rade, that there could've been Mr. Purvis's stuff."

"The foreman?"

"Yeah, Carter."

"Are you sure, Charlie?"

Krepp shook his head. "No, I ain't sure. But Carter wore a black bandanna, and I know he carried a pocketknife.

Used it all the time to whittle with or to clean out his horse's feet, like that. I never handled it, though. I couldn't say that that's the exact same knife or exact same bandanna, and I guess I never paid no mind to what kind of belt buckle he wore."

Weatherbee grunted. Krepp's information was hardly conclusive. Red was the most popular and common color for a bandanna, with blue running a distant second. Still, probably ten or fifteen percent of the cowboys one saw would be using the cheaper black bandannas. And a Barlow knife was about as unusual as dirt.

The dead man might have been Carter Purvis. He could as easily have been John Smith.

They walked back toward the hotel silently, each thinking his own thoughts, until a commotion on the sidewalk across the street drew their attention.

A storekeeper was throwing an Indian into the street, the eviction accompanied by shouts, curses, and a fair number of kicks to the Indian's ribs.

Charlie Krepp began to laugh. "Hey, Rade, that's the same Indian you pulled that Timmons fellow off of."

"Naw."

"It is. I swear it is."

Raider took another look. It was the same man, all right, withered arm and all. He shook his head. "That poor sonuvabitch has his troubles." He sighed. "In for a pint, in for a pound, I reckon. I'll be right back."

"What's this?" Doc asked.

Charlie explained while they trailed behind Raider crossing the street.

It was the same Indian, all right. He broke into a nearly toothless grin when he saw Raider and hardly paid any attention to the storekeeper who was still kicking him in the ribs.

"What the hell has he done this time?" Raider asked.

"I caught the red-livered son of a bitch stealing from my cracker barrel," the storekeeper complained. "See?" He bent and yanked the front of the Indian's tattered shirt open, popping the few buttons that had remained intact on the rag.

Half a pound of stale crackers spilled out onto the ground. The Indian immediately began scrambling with his good hand in an attempt to recover them.

"Okay," Raider said, "he was stealing crackers from you. Hell, the poor SOB is hungry, and he's got a family to feed. Let him have the damn crackers. And a sackful of flour, dried apples, shit like that. Okay?"

"Okay! Okay my ass," the storekeeper grumbled. "I'm not running some charity here."

Raider fished a coin from his pocket. "No charity. You *are* running a store here, right?"

The storekeeper grinned and took the coin. He also stopped kicking the Indian. "That's different."

Raider looked down at the Indian. He was about to deliver a lecture to the fellow, then realized that it would be a waste of breath. Fuck it. He'd done what he could. Any more and he'd be expected to take the bastard to raise, him and all his kin. He shut his mouth and went back to the hotel, with Charlie Krepp hurrying after him.

Weatherbee for some reason stayed behind. Probably wanted to do some shopping, Raider thought.

Though what anybody could find to buy in Wolf Point, well, that was Weatherbee's business, odd as it might be.

CHAPTER TWENTY-SIX

Doc topped the final rise and pulled his horse to a halt—
or Raider's horse, if anyone wanted to split hairs, since
Raider was the one who had rented the animal and from
whom Doc had borrowed it—and sat admiring the scene
that was spread out below him.

It was about as pretty a sight as he could remember seeing
in a very long time. The valley bottom held grass that was
belly deep to a fat cow, and beyond it were the Cypress
Hills of Saskatchewan, verdant and lovely.

On the hillside below, a small knot of blood red cows
grazed, while below them their calves slept nose to tail,
almost hidden in the tall grass. One cow stood guard over
the nursery while the others ate. Later some other mother
cow would take over the nursery duties so the current
babysitter could have lunch. Doc always found that trait
amusing and faintly amazing too. No one ever expected
sense from a cow, but sometimes they exhibited it.

Below the cattle, at the upper end of the emerald valley,
a group of men were at work building a stone house that
would protect them against the winter. Other men were
building pens for the cattle and the saddle horses.

It was a lovely scene. Peaceful. Pleasant. For a moment
Doc felt a twinge of envy. The men who were working

down there were carving for themselves a place of tranquility amid a sea of cares.

Doc took time to light an Old Virginia, then let the horse pick its way down the slope. The cattle merely looked at him as he passed, not bothering to scatter and run the way the leggy, range-bred longhorns of the south country would have done. These fat white-faced beasts were calmly domesticated.

As he came closer to the workmen, heads were raised, hammers and trowels were set aside. They were curious about him. He felt no sense of danger, though. None of these men was armed. No one reached for a gunbelt or a carbine. In fact, he could see no weapons anywhere in sight.

One of the men, a tall good-looking fellow with the bronze of working outdoors without a shirt, put down the handles of the barrow he had been wheeling, carrying a load of stone to the house builders. He pulled a red bandanna from his hip pocket, used it to wipe his hands, and then approached Doc with a smile on his face and his hand extended.

"Welcome," he said. "Light and set if you like."

"Thanks." Doc dismounted and tied the horse to a corral post that as yet had no rails attached. He shook hands with the man.

"John Sailor," the man introduced himself.

Doc smiled. Sailor. The name seemed logical. John Boatwright, John Sailor. Why not.

"I don't believe I caught your name," the man who called himself Sailor said.

"Oh, sorry. I was wool-gathering for a moment." Doc introduced himself.

"We can't offer you a roof quite yet, but there should be coffee on the fire over there."

"Thanks." Doc followed Sailor to the camp and took a seat on an upended log section that was being used as a stool. He accepted the cup of coffee Sailor poured. The rancher poured one for himself and sat also. "What brings you up this way, Mr. Weatherbee?"

"Allan Pinkerton wanted to make sure that things were

going well for a, uh, certain friend of his."

Sailor's eyes cut away from Doc's, and he seemed to be in thought for a moment. Likely deciding whether to try and bluff his way through or make the admission, Doc thought.

The decision was quickly reached. "How did you find us?" Sailor/Boatwright asked.

"It wasn't hard once I realized you'd come north. All the searching had been done to the south, of course. The direction everyone thought you were taking from the Timmons place."

Sailor grunted. He reached for his shirt pocket before he realized he was wearing no shirt, then got up and went to a pack lying on the ground to fetch the makings for a cigarette. He took his time about rolling and lighting it. When he had the quirly going he sighed. "I sure thought nobody saw us."

"Some Indians did," Doc told him. "I doubt they would bother to tell anyone else."

"They told you."

"Yes."

Sailor looked troubled. "We did nothing illegal, you know. The money was all mine. I just decided not to go back. There isn't anything wrong in that."

Doc raised an eyebrow questioningly. "Is Carter Purvis with you?"

Sailor sighed and examined the glowing tip of his cigarette. "No," he said. "Purvis is dead."

"I rather thought he might be."

Sailor hesitated for another moment. He raised his head and looked Doc in the eyes. "It was a fair fight, Mr. Weatherbee. I called him out, true, but it was a fair fight. Any of the boys would tell you that. They were all there. I hid nothing from them. And . . . they all knew the reason why I called Carter out."

He did not try to explain himself to Doc. But then, he did not have to, although he probably would not know that. Angela Boatwright. She was a round-heeled, expensive slut. Her interest in Purvis had been made plain enough. And

Doc had seen more than enough for himself to explain Boatwright's challenge to the man who had been filling his bed when Boatwright was absent.

Doc nodded. He didn't want to elaborate on his understanding of the situation any more than John Boatwright—John Sailor now—wanted to explain himself. The memories could not be pleasant for Boatwright.

"And the rest of the crowd?"

"They came with me. Most of those boys have been with me for a long time. They're a good crew. And good Lord, man, whatever you and Allan decide to do about me, don't let them get the boys in Dutch. They haven't done anything wrong."

"You left Krepp behind."

"Yeah. Thank God it worked out so good, him wanting to make that visit in Denver and everything. The rest of the boys didn't like him much. Couldn't trust him. He'd have blabbed it if he'd had any sniff at what was going on. Besides, he cheats at cards. We couldn't trust him, you see."

Raider had mentioned to Doc about the kid's luck at cards and how Rade had almost had trouble because of that. No wonder he was so lucky. And so susceptible to trouble.

"The rest of them came, though?" Doc asked.

Sailor nodded. "I began thinking it over back when I got the contract from Timmons. I stripped off every animal worth selling from the home place and brought them all north. Hell, I didn't want any of them for this new venture. The days of the big open range are about over. Max Timmons doesn't know that, but it's so. The future of the cattle business is in well-blooded stock managed under fence. I've been watching it come. And back home most of the range we used was open grass. I didn't actually own a tenth of it. Another few years and there won't be any open range left anywhere in Texas. It will take a while longer for that same thing to spread up this way, but it'll come."

"You've thought it out pretty carefully," Doc said.

"I had my reasons." He shrugged. "When the opportunity came, well, I made my decision. I don't regret it. Even now, Mr. Weatherbee, I have no regrets."

Sailor took a last drag on his cigarette and tossed the butt into the embers of the fire. "One thing I'd really appreciate," he said.

"What's that?"

"I've been thinking about this for the last little bit, since you got here, and I'm just not the kind who could raise his hand against someone who's in the right, even if you weren't working for a friend of mine. So I guess I've got no choice but to come with you. But I would ask that you not put any handcuffs on me. At least not where any of the boys can see. I've got some pride, you know. And they've been a good crew. Friends, not just employees. It would be hurtful if they saw me—"

"Whoa," Doc said.

"What?"

Doc smiled at him. "I came up here looking for a man named Boatwright. I don't believe I've found anyone by that name. And besides, Mr. Sailor, even if I did, as you said yourself, Boatwright has done nothing wrong in the States. He isn't wanted for anything as far as I know."

"Carter Purvis?"

"There are no charges outstanding that I know of in connection with Purvis. Has this Purvis done something that he would be wanted by the law?"

Sailor blinked.

"For your information, Mr. Sailor, there was a body found north of Wolf Point. The body was not identified. The cause of death is unknown. The, uh, man, whoever he was, could well have died of natural causes.

"I see," Sailor said. He began rolling another smoke. "That body that was found north of Wolf Point, Mr. Weatherbee. Is that what pointed you in that direction?"

"It started me thinking," Doc admitted. "It didn't seem reasonable that no one had reported seeing Boatwright south of the Timmons ranch. Then there was that body found in the wrong direction. An Indian who owed my partner confirmed it."

" 'our partner?"

Doc nodded. "He's back in Wolf Point now. I told him I wanted to ride out and check a hunch. He doesn't know why I'm here. Young Krepp and, uh, Mrs. Boatwright are with him."

Pain, and perhaps regret as well, showed in John Sailor's pale blue eyes. "Yes. Angela." He smiled sadly. "I can't honestly say that I'll miss her. But it was damn sure interesting, Weatherbee. It was damn sure interesting while it lasted."

"I can imagine."

Sailor flicked a match aflame and lighted his cigarette. "What will you tell Allan?"

"What do you want me to tell him?" Doc countered.

Sailor smiled. "The best thing would be to tell him nothing at all. But I suppose that wouldn't do, would it?"

"No," Doc agreed.

"Angela has probably run up a bill with him, too. I wouldn't want to stiff him for that."

"Mrs. Boatwright contracted the bill. As far as I know she would be the one expected to pay it."

A slow grin crossed Sailor's face. "To tell you the truth, Weatherbee, she might not honor that bill. Even if she wanted to. She, uh, doesn't have near as much in that fancy Louisiana bank as she thinks she does."

"Oh."

Sailor shrugged. And smiled again.

It *was* his money, Doc reminded himself. And Angela Boatwright was hardly deserving of any consideration. The fact that the man had chosen to leave her anything at all was remarkable. Damned well honorable even. Doc decided to drop the subject.

"I have a suggestion," Doc said.

"Yes?"

"John Boatwright—if I could find him, that is—might want to send his old friend a message that he is doing well and that he has moved. He, uh, would not have to give Allan a new address if he didn't wish to. And I suspect Allan would be grateful if Mr. Boatwright were to pay the agency's bill for services that were rendered unnecess

"You would convey that message from Mr. Boatwright?"

"I would," Doc said.

"What about John Sailor?"

"It seems to me that John Sailor is free, white, and twenty-one. The agency would have no interest in him. Neither would anyone else that I know of."

Sailor looked relieved. "I thank you, Mr. Weatherbee."

"On behalf of Mr. Boatwright, I presume."

"Yes. On behalf of Mr. Boatwright. And now if you would excuse me, sir, I believe I have a letter to write. Would you be offended if the letter were sealed?"

"Of course not, Mr. Sailor."

"Thank you."

CHAPTER TWENTY-SEVEN

Doc let himself into the hotel room. He wanted a bath. His clothes were filthy from the dust of the travel. His saddlebags, containing a bulky letter from John Boatwright to Allan Pinkerton, were slung over his shoulder.

He unlocked the hotel room door and shoved it open. Immediately a broad grin came over his beard-stubbled face. His timing could not have been better.

"Hello," he said cheerfully.

Raider blanched and turned his head to give Doc a vicious scowl. The red-haired girl who was lying beneath him squealed and tried to hide her face in Raider's sweaty chest.

"Damn you, Weatherbee!" Raider bellowed. He jumped off the bed, giving Doc a somewhat better view of the comely lass, and came at Doc with a roar.

Raider was at somewhat of a disadvantage, though, being naked. And Doc had left the room door standing open.

A lady passing in the corridor shrieked with alarm and looked like she was going to faint—which her companion, a tall and belligerent-looking gentleman, did not appreciate in the slightest.

Raider blushed and dived back toward the protection of the bedsheets, but by then the red-haired girl, still squealing, had wrapped herself in the sheet and was lying on the floor behind the far side of the bed.

"Nice to see you, Rade," Doc said pleasantly. He put his saddlebags down and sauntered casually to close the door to the hallway. "Been doing all right for yourself?" He peered over the edge of the bed and waved to the girl on the floor. Her face was now quite as red as her hair.

His moment of joy was interrupted when Raider's shoulder slammed into Doc's belly, doubling him over and sending both of them tumbling to the floor in a flurry of flying arms, legs, and fists.

Considerably later, over drinks intended to kill the aches of their assorted bruises, Doc brought Raider more or less up to date.

"Boatwright sent a letter to Allan by way of a man named Sailor," he said. "The letter's sealed, so I don't know what's in it. But the fact remains, the assignment is a washout. Boatwright isn't missing, and no one stole that money. So we don't have a case anymore."

"I'll be damned," Raider said.

"Probably," Doc agreed willingly. "Where is your shadow?"

"Who? Oh. Charlie. He found some filly about to take off downriver on a steamer. Some gal with big tits and no brains. And she was dressed like her daddy was prob'ly rich. I ain't seen Charlie since."

"And Mrs. Boatwright?"

"She's still got her room at the hotel, but nobody's seen her use the room for two, three days now. Nobody seems to give a shit. In fact, the folks at the hotel seem right glad to have her elsewhere.

"Where is she?"

"How should I know?" Raider asked innocently.

"The woman has been the Pinkerton Agency's responsibility. I know you're a lazy cretin, Raider, but you aren't *that* bad an operative. Where is she?"

Raider grinned at him. "Shacked up with a riverboat gambler named Ed Farley. They're a right handsome couple, too."

"Rich, is he?"

Raider grinned again. "The man looks rich. He dresses rich. He damn sure acts rich. But then I reckon he figures she's rich enough for the both of them."

Raider did not really understand why Weatherbee got such a tremendous kick out of that information.

Hell, he thought, the woman was rich. Wasn't she? He shook his head. There were times when he just didn't understand Weatherbee. Probably the old bastard's mind was failing.

Raider looked at his partner across the table, then reached up to feel his jaw. The damn thing sure was aching. He owed Doc for that one, all right. There was no doubt it was a debt he would have to repay. The question was only when, not whether.